SLEEPWALKERS

"When the atmosphere is soporific, somnambulists are plunged into jeopardy." Manyika Thomodia

Manyika Thomodia

2020
TALNET INDEPENDENT PUBLISHERS
HARARE ZIMBABWE

DEDICATION

To my father – your faith in the value of education has at last been justified.

To Brian Zabhura and Mr Kichini- your illuminating advice gave this book its breath of life.

To Pamela Manyika – I appreciate the moral and Financial Support as well as your unflinching criticism.

CHAPTER ONE

Part One

I could see from afar the state of the School as I proceeded towards my first government job. The Education inspectors had told me that a remote School is ideal for someone with little or no experience like me.

'I've got the job.' the euphoria of securing a relief teaching position was inexplicable. I have been offered a chance to redeem my dying self-esteem.

Exclusively, intoxicated with the excitement, I was so absorbed in a sort of a reverie that I lost the track of time and its passage. Ironically it was a long haul from the bus station to the School. It was no easy affair descending and ascending the mountainous areas of Chimanimani. A huge suitcase and a satchel were practically killing my shoulders.

I passed a dip tank, a police base; a small clinic probably staffed with one qualified nurse and some miserable grocery shops.

As I approached the school, the first feature I noticed was a rusty sign post perched on a lemon tree written in block letters, ***'WELCOME TO OXFORD SECONDARY SCHOOL.'*** There was a two hundred meter orchard if not a plantation of lemon trees which could make one to ponder whether the School had plans to manufacture lemonade or it was just a lemon plantation.

My eyes were drawn to the School gate; there stood two men and a woman. The three introduced themselves as Mr Zabhura, Mr Chesa and Miss Mombeshora.

Mr. Zabhura was a lanky man who was dark brown in complexion, with darting eyes. He looked very intelligent and from my own point of view, obviously he was a History Teacher. I bet that I was observant. Mr Chesa the leader of the pack had a bullet shaped head with a shiny bald, with a huge smile plastered on his face when he saw me approaching, appeared mature enough to be one of the senior teaching staff. Miss Mombeshora a young charming lady of my age between nineteen and twenty two seemed to be on her TP 'Teaching Practice'. Cladded in a Mutare Teachers College tracksuit, she was light in complexion, naturally beautiful, also realized her sweet voice had a certain musicality whilst her mouth was curved with a bright smile. An English student teacher I bet.

It was almost mid-day now when I arrived at the school, the three accompanied me ceremoniously to the Teachers residence. We headed far west to uniformly built single quarters where I was to reside. There was a round neatly thatched kitchenette attached to a square brick walled bedroom under asbestos.

Mr Chesa showed me the house and henceforth precedes the inspection of the rooms like a museum tour guide. Though sparsely furnished, the furniture looked polished. A single wood framed bed painted brown, a wooden arm chair, brown painted tiny dressing table and a small desk in the bedroom. A tiny fitted kitchen unit, a stool and a fire place at the midpoint of the kitchenette. The rooms looked pretty and aptly eyeing them appreciatively. After the three had left I unpacked my bags, spread the bed and took a nap.

The dying sun casted its golden rays through the window. Being lonely I decided to walk around to acquaint myself with the surroundings and work place as well as refreshing. Tomorrow Tuesday being the Schools official opening day, it was essential to perceive the environment, classrooms, toilets, School grounds, assembly point, the administration block etc.

The school appeared to be old with only three plastered but unpainted classroom blocks which were built during the Rhodesian government. From the entrance gate, only twenty yards was the administration block with three classrooms facing the teachers residence juxtaposed with form two (2) block facing east and a garden of flowers in between. The form three and four block was adjacent to the two facing north. Without the services of the guide this time around, I managed to drink into the School's state. It seems not to have been built at all but created in the beginning of primeval.

Almost dusk I returned to my place. I had to prepare for tomorrow's business. Darkness was coming down quickly.

I was busy contemplating on how best I would introduce myself to the pupils and consequently conduct successful first lessons, when there was a kind of shocking discreet knock on the door. I wasn't expecting any visitor. Wondering who it could be, I walked on bare feet from the bedroom into the rotunda to the door and opened it.

"Ooh! Shylet Paradzai!" I yelled with astonishment. She giggled and blushed. "What are you doing here?" I asked her quizzically.

I knew Shylet from Harvard High School where she was our Head prefect studying A'level upper six commercials. She studied Business studies, Accounts and Geography. Although I was studying Arts in Shona, Literature in English and Geography at lower six, we could meet for discussions because of the common subject. I made friends with her since High School. We shared crucial information. She was a very attractive girl of more than medium height who wore no make-up and had a face most men would desire to categorize as enticing rather than beautiful. She was a very smart, organized, humble and intelligent girl.

"So sorry to bother you so late Thomodia." she said in a voice that was cool and controlled. "I couldn't resist coming to see you from the moment I got wind of your arrival here." she added in a deep and pleasant voice.

"Then I think you better come in dearest." I replied lively and opened the door wide and stepped aside to let her in and ushered her the way straight through to the bedroom really puzzled as to why she was calling on me so late.

"It has been a long time. I came to see you Thomo um…" she paused. All at once I began to feel a little uneasy. There was an awkward and almost embarrassing silence. I motioned her to the chair, then she continued sitting on the chair. "Ugh I really missed you Manyika. So how are you and where have you been perched in this country? Ooh okay, let me start by congratulating you about…"

"Yeah it was no easy getting the job." I interjected, pulling out the tiny desk and sitting on top of it. "But I deserved it, you really know that I used to have *galas* at School." I said humorously.

"Oh yes! Real *pungwes*." she replied enthusiastically half giggling.

During our High School days we termed whole night reading with less or without sleeping a *gala* or *pungwe* derived from all night traditional festivals or *bira* for rainmaking ceremonies or for any appeasement of evil spirits. In that particular case, having endured an all-night reading *gala* was grade 'A's or 'B's pass making ceremony, but depended on one's strength in psychological and mental faculties. Some were overpowered by the evil spirits and retire to sleep during those night studying rituals. Part of those who managed to circumvent, could come to School red eyed, looking dejected and most probably would be summoned and apprehended by the sleep spirit right in the middle of crucial lessons. Not only at one point do I remember Mr Mahundi our A' level class Teacher complaining on us due to trivial *galas*, really worthless *pungwes*. Alas, imagine the teacher's frustration when the whole class is dozing in a crucial lesson. Aye, what matters the most were the final results. *Galas* worked in my favor but for Kunyadai a close friend of mine it didn't avail despite all his valiant endeavors.

He got nothing out of it. We referred him the *Gala Champ* or the *owl*. He couldn't sleep. He had information, to the extent of reciting the whole textbook and its page numbers but consequently failed final examinations. I wondered why he flopped. Maybe he took a nap during examination or the heaving datum led to his cerebral explosion and henceforth lost his logic.

I thought; reading and grasping the right information and concepts, acquiring tactical question answering skills and spare enough time to sleep as well as refreshing are of paramount importance to a student. Otherwise just reading for the sack of reading is sleepwalking as far as education is concerned. A student should be capable of reading behind the lines especially in examinable literature novels. It becomes a worthless *gala* whilst fumbling.

During this stream of thought, Shylet enquired anxiously. "What are you gathering about? You experienced tormenting *galas*?"

"No! No not at all." I said with a short bark I had meant to laugh.

"You did Shona and English *lits*, I'm aware it's a cumbersome combination Thomo. All those novels!" she protested.

"T'was easy, I'm a bookworm." I said reassuringly.

"All those novels! Both Shona and English set books!" she expostulated.

"Not a bad combination dear, it's really apt for serious bookworms of my caliber…. Yep t'was a heavy load but not that much." I admitted condescendingly.

"I think you're also going to be a writer. I know your potentialities and it's my wish"

A Writer? I wondered what I would write about. Crime, love, politics, fiction or what? All the same I couldn't imagine myself writing anything.

She've to thrust herself in my shoes first, whatever the shoe size and then realize how mammoth the task is. Nonetheless, I amazed myself by answering tuned in the same frequency of hers, as if my onward mouth had a mind of its own "My dear friend, I've submitted your wish before the High Court of my heart and ... your wish is my command." She was now wreathed in smiles.

As we talked, a great curiosity was preying on my mind. I decided to switch the subject, in a tone of affectionate curiosity. "What are you doing here at Oxford?" I asked her.

"I'm also a temporary teacher just like you dear." she replied with a pitying smile sitting on her face.

"Ho!" I exclaimed.

"My parents could no longer afford to pay for my Post Grad, so temporary teaching is the only option available. But um ... Oxford Secondary School umm ... this Mandima area ugh!" Without a shadow of doubt, she wasn't contended with the teaching occupation particularly in this outlying area. She was originally city bred. But for me I didn't mind because I was a soldier enough and also already in cloud nine. "I came here last term and I'm teaching Accounts and Commerce form two and three. Those lout and obstinate adolescences!" she paused and a faraway look came to her face. I looked at her puzzled, and in due course she continued. "I had a hard time suppressing my sobs the first day I came here. The area is still full of primitives." she said.

One must never lose an opportunity of acquiring knowledge. I desperately needed an insight, so I asked her some questions pertaining to the School, what made her nearly sob? But my dear friend refused to gasp out her story. She only said, "You will see it for yourself sir."

Though I had been deeply interested in the teaching job, I felt a vague of dissatisfaction, the cause of which I could not quite make out, maybe initiated by my failure to coax her. The words 'lout and obstinate adolescences' chilled my heart. I felt utterly discouraged. A bad School? I repelled the painful thought with all my strength and said, "I've my own methods and I'm equal to the task Shylet." I adopted a stern tone "And ... anyway, tomorrow is second term Schools official opening day. I will be teaching English language form one and two ... juniors right!" I said.

"My dear friend it won't hold water that they're juniors. Most of the children and their parents are in pitch darkness." she said

"I will instill remarkable discipline into the students"

She looked at me perplexed, "how will you do that?"

"I will edify them humility and morals. I'll shape them into better students and spank the indiscipline ones." She didn't look convinced and I began to feel exasperated, "don't worry I'll knock some senses in them, I possess the tactics."

"Splendid" she said and grinned. The tragic reality was that I didn't know how I would perform those miracles. "Why did you opt for Oxford Secondary School?" she enquired.

I replied hypocritically: "I never asked them to." Then a memory flashed through my mind. During temporary teacher recruitment at Chimanimani District Education offices the previous day, some of the shortlisted candidates rejected the School citing various reasons. At first I had an opportunity to opt for Lydia Chimonyo Girls High School but later chose Oxford considering a lesser competition. Nevertheless I didn't won the post uncontested. I excelled at High School and came out the highest. My results were convincing enough but faced stiff challenge from this girl Lizzy a former Mutambara Mission High School student. We had equal A' level points with same grades from the same subjects; somehow I narrowly outperformed her at O' level.

"I'm very glad you came here Thomo, with your friendship a new life begins for me." and she smiled indulgently.

"But don't chew up yourself. You will soon get your niche, I'm telling you, very soon! Remember, delay is not denial." I had said prophetically. There was no vestige of doubt in my mind that my friendship with her was now rekindling like never before. She nodded appreciatively when she saw the look on my face.

"Aren't you hungry?" I asked a hedging sort of question.

"If you brought pizza, I am hungry." she giggled.

In a trice I took a food warmer basin from my satchel and two coincidental half liter mango juice bottles for both of us. We devoured the scrumptious rice and chicken my mum had prepared for me. We had a juicy oiled conversation of our past experiences at Harvard High.

For tomorrow's breakfast, she volunteered to prepare potato chips for I had bought potatoes along the way. I sorted the gas stove methodically whilst she peeled the potatoes.

Aren't my eyes lying? I could not believe my own eyes. I could feel them bugging as if ready to pop out of their sockets. Is it optical illusion? Whimsically, I stood up and clamped her drumstick arm with my hand reminiscing on how I used to sermonize her during our High School days on morality and condemnation of spurious looks. She stared at me with uncomprehending eyes. Her false look made anger climb up inside me.

"Yellow bonnie!" I barked.

It seems as if Shylet has just migrated from another planet. Her face was as yellow as a lemon, but her knuckles were originally black as charcoal. The shapely figure of hers was jammed into a pair of blue slacks; probably her legs too resembled the original skin color. Fortuitous enough, I observed her dark pinna which gave a tinge to the initial complexion. Human skin color blocking! I wanted to burst out, to explode into maniac laughter at the absurdity of It all, but I did not. I also wondered why I didn't notice it at the very first time she came in. Maybe it was due to a nostalgic cloud of High School life. Actually one never notices such things quickly unless of course if one is of a lust-oriented mind.

Without wanting to bother her, I said "this is the epitome of beauty." she blushed pink with pride. "Has anybody told you before what a pretty lady you are?" I asked icing the cake and further lightening the atmosphere.

"Hey bro! I don't remember." she replied, with her voice higher than the hissing blue flame from the gas stove and the noise of sizzling chips in a frying pan. In this case I managed to make her elated. "I *wanna* look like Nicky Minaj." she said gaily with a radiant smile.

The mentioning of Nicky Minaj triggered an emotional avalanche within me, because that change doesn't just happen like rain, "sometimes dreams cannot transform into reality. Maybe you're unaware that Nicky's are suspected to have no real assets." I said quite candidly. She somehow gave me the sort of look that woman gives when she hasn't cooked an answer to an argument, but which some wise gives you the feeling that you have lost the argument anyway.

I shrugged and casted my eyes at her once more. Ooh she had really changed! Well sculpted legs led into enticingly swelling thighs and voluptuous hips. She was now a lady with finely chiseled curvaceous features similar to Nicky Minaj a gorgeous American hip-hop chanter. Nicky is said to have gone under the knife. Upon realizing that blacks envy the white skin; chemicals, lotions, tablets were made to enhance the black skin. But why did our sisters not ponder about it all that under the bait there is a hook? What's the demon sneakily got into women these days? They all itch to look white! Isn't Shylet also in pitch darkness? Does she know the adverse consequences?

She was staring at me impassively, enduring all my scrutiny with an admirable calmness and not even once did she bat an eye lid. Finally she broke the silence. "Lots of women are doing it all the time. If you throw a stone at a group of women there's a high probability of hitting a bleached one."

Does company mean security? I wondered. "Are you aware of the consequences or your mind is just unconscious?" I asked, and then totted. "It seems you also went under the knife and you're swallowing tablets to enhance your complexion! What's the problem with just looking African … umm I mean natural?" my voice was a little sharper than I had intended. She then peeped at me coyly through the mascara palings of her supplementary lashes. "As a result, some end up going under mastectomy due to malfunction of the implants. Do you know prosthesis? Anyway my friend, are you aware of skin cancer? Imagine how you would appear like when you reach our grandmother's age."

She almost stamped her foot in exasperation. "Enough! Enough Thomo!" she fumed and added. "You once said this is the epitome of beauty."

"But you're a fake *yellow bonnie*" I said and busted into a provocative laugher that later died somewhere in my guts.

"You're now mortifying me! Okay I've had enough of you. Good night. Bye!" she said harshly and made a movement of being about to get up.

Realizing that my missile had knocked the target, I tried to quench the fire. "Wait! Control yourself and calm down for Christ's sake. What's chewing on you? Spill it! What's on your mind?" I asked rhetorically.

"You're not a good friend Thomo, wasn't there any better way of telling me?" she accused and enquired.

I realized the name *'fake yellow bonnie'* did something within her. "I wasn't malevolent; it's just a frank talk. I regret that I frustrated you *Besty*"

She cringed. "You forgot at school I used to exonerate your misdeeds. We had a stronger bond than the umbilical cord. Do you want to weaken it? Sometimes your openness and criticism unnerves me." She made a gesture of hopelessness or frustration; it was difficult to tell which one.

"I'm sorry, I regret the blunder. But I think you heard my point. Treat your skin and body in a sacrosanct way."

She nodded morosely. "I never accounted the consequences, what I just craved for is to appear more gorgeous."

God forbid! She is educated but why is she unconscious on such matters? But how could she? Maybe cosmetic magazines, television or social media had blind folded her brains. "Okay Shylet, but guard against trying to justify the unjustifiable. Being *yellow* doesn't guarantee you a good marriage or a successful life ..."

"But I've a degree Thomo! I'm not a beauty without brains." she attested.

"A degree in Cosmetology?"

"No! Bachelor of Commerce in Marketing Management"

I decided not to further rub salt into her wounds. "I've the perfect icing for your cake dear ... umm try natural herbs for Christ's sake they're salubrious."

She blinked as if she had been interrupted from some brief reverie. "No I already used tables and injections, if I erroneously mix up, I'll end up looking like a gorilla." We bused into laughter. Now she smiled radiantly and I knew the tension had gone out of the atmosphere between us. I also knew she was never able to hold a grudge. Shylet is very weak in the grudge holding muscle.

Now it was 9:30pm. She had finished frying potato chips and had already turned off the sibilant gas stove. We had netted enough. I accompanied her to her house just few yards from mine.

When I came back, my mind was drawn in a thought. Shylet had really changed her appearance but not a natural change at all. I remember very well at School she made no passes at the boys or men, and they attempted no serious shots at her, making her reasonably unique. But now she spent a lot to enhance her appearance in a bid to lure wealthy men. Perhaps driven by the love of money, *shagi, mula, bag gwalangwa* etc. they call it with all sorts of names these days. But biblically money is referred to as the root of all evil.

Bleaching causes terribly disgusting effects. Others end up looking like leopards with spotted skin. Be it cosmetic surgery, injections or tables used, they ensue early mortality, thus dicing with death. Deformity is considered lucky, one buttock bigger than the other! The powdered ones are better for their fright is mostly on rainfall as it might wash and spoils all the endeavors. These days you meet unsophisticated girls with the so called *yellow faces* and coal black toes, it's absurd! Isn't it? It's now a diluted culture isn't it?

Not only woman but also some feminine boys are doing it unscrupulously. Let me not delve into the issue of the one outrageous tatelicious. However those who impeccably follow the instructions on using, or even after liposuction or facelift can manage to maintain an undoubtedly good shaped body and skin to the extent of one requiring divine intervention on distinguishing between natural and bleached. It's very sacrilegious altering our God given sanctity ethos as Africans. The end results lead to loss of self-esteem within that jaundice. You look good for some few years then the nasty effects would bulldoze that beauty for the fruits will ripen. Others end up developing a fester terracotta skin like about to get rotten.

A blissful matrimony is not guaranteed because of being euphonically known as *yellow bonnie*. I don't know why yellow bonnie fanatics are blind folded by the fanciful beatific of owning one. Even callow country girls in their salad days frittering the sense of identity are masquerading as from posh families unabashed, but when she happens to speak huh! a real Ndau or Samanyika with a horse coarse or masculine voice above it all will suddenly emerge.

Aren't they solar eclipses? It's a ubiquitous *yellow fever* that has plagued our black African continent.

Envious girls should be forewarned and awakened not to make decisions one would ever live to regret. Even the naturally light ones should bear in mind that a successful life can't come all on a silver platter. Black beauties accompanied by awake brains are more preferred at the expense of deceitful *yellow* narrow- minded narcissists who lack essentials just like the devoid of any meaning in the mumbled muttering of a somnambulist.

A lot of African girls are lacking a long range view due to Westernization which has proved to be the chief contributor of the moral bankruptcy and decadence that is prevailing especially among us youths.

Rousing myself from the muse, I threw some quick glances round the room, devoured a handful of potato chips, gulped a glass of water and retire to bed. But with a question hanging on my mind; why our African sisters are killing their natural beauty?

CHAPTER TWO

Part One

As I was walking towards the assembly point from the Headmaster's office after I submitted my assumption of duty papers, I could easily see that students were all looking at me. Most of the students were still coming to the assembly point. Some were wearing shoes whilst others had no shoes at all. I was then surprised to see a High school which allows students to come to school with no shoes.

In the next to no time, students were now standing at the assembly point according to their respective classes, starting with form ones at the front lines and form fours at the back.

Mr Zabhura addressed the assembly and made salutations. The Headmaster Mr Chimeri didn't turn up because of the chilling weather. He had told me he went under an operation recently so he didn't want to be exposed to cold weather.

Mr Chesa the Deputy Head introduced me to the students. There were wild whistles and ululations from the juniors with their faces iced with pride. I remained dump, peaceful and smiling. Some were still piercing whistles, and it stopped at the word of command.

The assembly was then cut short because of the rains which were now starting to fall. All the teaching staff members, fast trotted to the Administration block where the staff room was located. All the other teachers took their places and promptly I spotted a vacant chair in between Miss Mombeshora and Shylet. It was a perfect place sandwiched by two beautiful ladies *fake yellow bonnie* to my left and a lighter black beauty to my right side.

With no time, Mr Chimeri entered into the staff room hurriedly, in a rapid walk which seemed to imply he had little time to waste in walking. But his frowning face exhibited that he was experiencing operation pains.

We found ourselves now talking in whispers as if we were in the exam room.

He then put his big diary on the table, and said "welcome back all of you!" whilst unwinding his scarf.

I promptly classed him among the aged. He had a big body and a biggish nose advantageously shortened by his spectacles. He was a very serious man of little or no humor. His speech proved that he was a real professional man as he diligently exhorted all of us to work up to standards. He also introduced me formally to all other teachers and invited me again to his office soon after the meeting. Although I was a novice, in my modest opinion the meeting was just ordinary as it was a mere emphasis on reviving the school standards that had drastically declined. Mr Chimeri also lamented on the very poor pass rate and urged all especially exam class teachers to exert extra effort. After the conclusion of the meeting I followed him to his office, just a few steps from the staff room.

"Well! Mr Manyika Thom … Thoumm … Thomodia!" he struggled to pronounce my first name. "Huh! What does your name really mean?" he asked anxiously.

"No doubt" I replied.

"Okay there's no doubt that you're going to execute your duties excellently. Here are your scheme books and attendance register." he handed me the books. "You're form one B class teacher, I hold you responsible for that class Mr Manyika." I happened to be a nodding acquaintance. "But we've a disciplinary challenge at this school. I expect you to cooperate and endeavor to instill discipline into our children." He said removing his jacket to wear a yarn knitted jersey. I noticed the blue shirt he was wearing; washed so many times and it was now as thin as a tissue paper. Maybe he wasn't able to afford new ones because of a meager salary also exacerbated by the prevailing economic hardships. Buying new clothes is considered a luxury due to the sky rocketing prices of basic commodities.

"But don't eat your own eggs!"

"I'm sorry, I didn't get what you're saying Sir?" I asked.

He smiled without malice. "We've so many pretty girls at this School. Don't attempt to coerce love! It costs you the job. Better to hunt in the staff room if need be."

"What?" I shot back at him.

"It's better to be hanged for a sheep than a lamp. Do you know that adage and what it means?"

"Yes I do" I was not in the mood for a lecture, no matter how right he was.

He looked at me nodding his head. "I head you almost cohabitated Miss Paradzai yesterday. That's why I say keep casting your nets at big fish within the staff room. Don't ever attempt at shallow pools" he said alongside with some avuncular looks. There wasn't any room for doubt that he was also deeply questioning my moral and spiritual fiber. He sat there half smiling at me whilst I wondered how I was supposed to answer that one. I implicitly knew that someone spied on us yesterday but it seemed the person didn't dropped on us because our conversation proved there wasn't any intimacy. His thoughts were merely fallacious.

"Miss Paradzai is just my High School friend."

"Which School?" he asked.

"Harvard High School." I answered.

He seemed to ponder for a minute, his face deep in concentration. "How's Mr Kichini? Well, I'm now confident that you were taught and groomed very well in English. He has vast knowledge in English. We all knew him at English teachers workshops and seminars." he said.

I was very glad he knew my A' level Literature in English mentor. "He is very fine sir." I replied with a happy tone.

"Okay go and mark your attendance register and check the time table for your lessons. We don't have to put any black mark against your record, so execute your duties carefully."

"Okay, thank you sir." I scrammed from the office and went straight to form one 'B' classroom, the second door of the block.

As I got into the classroom, students stood up and said in chorus, "good morning sir!" they said in unison as if they had rehearsed It a million times during the just ended holiday.

"Good morning to you all. You may all sit down." Quickly I had a pulsating anger because the classroom was looking like a pigsty. "This classroom is very dirty!" I barked. "Why don't you use your senses? Don't you have senses all of you? You could have swept the room clean even before going to the assembly point. After marking the register, I want all of you to make this classroom very tidy!" They just stared fixedly at me.

I made the introduction after disengaging myself from the rage and I marked the attendance register. The only absent student was Nadia, other forty one students were present.

"I want you to sweep and mop this room. Class monitor and monitress you're the supervisors. You have to beat the clock, so do it as quickly as possible"

I heard a girl's voice from the back of the room saying, "sir! Nadia our class monitress is absent!"

"Where is she? Is she sick? Or she just enjoyed and extended the holiday?"

"No! She is married!"

"Married!" I exclaimed. The whole class busted into a laugh stopping dead at the word of command. Early marriage! I quickly casted my eyes at the girls occupying front chairs trying to justify the possibility. They were bigger girls. One could class them between form three and form four. They were well fattened girls maybe because of good eating. One filled the whole chair without leaving any space at either sides. After the observation I blurted, "who married her?" as if I knew the whole Mandima area.

"Douglas the bus driver!" the girl replied.

I happened to remember Douglas a polygamous Omnibus driver. He ferried me the previous day from Cashel Valley to Mandima. I occupied the front seat in his bus when he gasped out his story along the way. He said to be in possession of four wives and a recent fifth one who eloped leaving school without a solid reason. She wasn't pregnant as he said. "But only the fact that I'm an omnibus driver chums. I'm not even the owner of the vehicle."

"But you two were in love?" I enquired.

"Yes chum, but she wasn't pregnant. She just eloped; maybe she anticipated a better life. So ... umm I married her at the end."

"You paid lobola? Was she aware that you already have other four wives before the elopement?"

"Yes she was. The bad part of It is that she is of an underage ... I received a phone call from the police inspector this morning. He needs me for questioning. Maybe I'll end up being thrown behind bars."

"Umm it's a serious case bro!" I said in a shaky voice. He wore an old brown torn sleeveless shirt, his navel outside implying he was failing to make ends meet. It seems he got all the wives just by being a driver and now the future of his polygamous family was now hanged by a thread due to the recruitment of an underage which he added to a lot. A ridiculous love pentagon! He tried to reveal squabbles among his wives en route but I turned on a deaf ear to his verbal diarrhorrea. He should carry his own cross because of his somnolence.

I didn't ask him why he resorted to school girls of his daughter's age, he proved to be more than the word foolish. He was in hot soup and he looked dejected, he lost concentration several times and he shifted his gears as if he was grinding his teeth. From my own panoramic point of view, his life could have been better if he chose monogamy and maintained only one wife.

Some bus drivers are promiscuous; they braggingly claim that they can't live the whole year with one woman like a calendar. They change women the way they shift vehicle gears. It's very disheartening. They don't think of the consequences. There's HIV and AIDS, unplanned pregnancies, disjoined families and also *Police Ahead.*

I threw some quick furtive glances at Douglas saying in my mind 'press accelerator bro, the Police inspector is waiting for you.' He noticed the fusillade glances and then I asked comically "what are the ingredients of diesel?"

"I don't know chum. Maybe there's ethanol something like that …" he paused for a moment. "Why did you ask that question chum? I'm a mere driver not an engineer."

"The smell of diesel woos women." We busted into a non-provocative laughter.

"Yeah they love motor vehicles," he said.

"They get obsessed too."

"One of my friends once said if monkeys were given money and cars, we could find a lot of women in mountains and forests," he said jocundly. I laughed at it, realizing that Douglas was one of the monkeys but a poor one and his polygamous home was the forest where this school dropout girl has resorted to. He was ugly as something from the darker ages. His eyes were like finely whetted daggers. A monkey!

It's unethical to have a love relationship with a school child; I realized the future of that girl was thrown into jeopardy. Maybe she was too smitten but she could have done better by deciding to complete school first and henceforth find better boys out there. Dropping school because of a bus driver isn't' a laudable idea. Maybe the school lacked proper education on these issues but that's the role of parents too. Zimbabwean government doesn't condone early marriages and its laws criminalize against it.

I don't know why school girls are also in such drowsiness. Can you imagine! Nadia knew that Douglas had four wives already and he was of the same age with her father. She didn't realize that one can't live the whole life blissfully eating zap nacks. Thus fantasy! Education should be trusted first as the priority.

After this stream of thought, I glanced back again at the girls sitting at the front row of the class and realized Chiedza the biggest one occupying the whole chair, maybe she was next in line. Her lips were red, having been dipped in a paper of tomato zap nacks. Surely there's need for a holistic approach in order to eradicate the proliferating early marriages. I tried to find an answer. "Why was she married at such a tender age?"

A boy's voice from the back replied, "She loved things!" and another one, "she was of a big body!" their answers were not startling. Maybe the big bodies are being caused by the food we eat these days. Some few years ago, a form one girl couldn't fill the whole chair, her buttocks were only concentrated at the center leaving enough spaces to comfortably accommodate for instance a small lunch box and a mathematical set at both sides.

A study by the institute for Family Studies also demystified that girls who get up married younger are prone to die earlier as they experience lots of complications during childbirth.

"Okay children, it's not good to get married so early. You've to finish High school first and you'll find better suitors at Colleges and Universities out there. So who is our Class Monitor?"

In chorus they all answered, "Simplicio Fundirwa!" I gave Simplicio the task of monitoring that everyone does a part in tiding both floors and windows. I trotted back to the staff room to prepare my schemes of work as well as checking on the time table for my lessons. Usually the first day was for putting things in order as well as introducing myself to my classes.

At the reception was a beautiful clerk. "Hie Mr Manyika," she waved as I was about to enter into the staff room.

"Hie Christwish, I thought you were very busy so I didn't want to bother you," I said stepping back to the reception.

"No I'm not busy, only few students have paid their school fees so I don't have much to do." She said with a smile displaying her teeth out. "The clerk's job isn't much, especially at this small school …" she paused after we heard footsteps from Headmaster's office.

"Mr Manyika! Assume class teacher's role in form four 'A' their class teacher Mr Mupanda is attending a sick relative, he'll be back in three days' time" he instructed. I remained rooted wondering why he didn't bring the attendance register book. "Just go and mark the register! Christwish won't go anywhere; you can see her after work. She can even fry your potato chips better." Mr Chimeri said satirically and sanctimoniously going back to his office. I remained puzzled. Christwish managed a small simper and patted her carefully crimped head. She swung round her seat and gave me the attendance register book without saying any word.

"Headship doesn't mean dictatorship." I humorously whispered and she laughed. Her strong white teeth went with the hearty laugh she fetched up from her guts. She had round plump cheeks and her big, high bosomed figure was handsome.

There were very few students in form four 'A' classroom, but the room was immaculate. They greeted me, their faces showing great excitements. I had little time to waste, so I began with girls, calling out their names audaciously and the bearers of the names professing their presence by audibly replying 'present!' only at once I was unpleasantly surprised to hear the reply "pregnant!" after calling out the name Mavis. It was a boy's voice. These are rhyming words 'pregnant' and 'present' is It auditory illusion? I thought my ears had cheated me.

"Mavis!" I barked now with a louder voice.

"Pregnant!" this time the reply came from a girl's voice from the back row.

I grimaced and scoffed at the imbecility of the two. "Mavis stand up!" she stood up. Actually she sat at the front row. A pretty girl with a flat tummy but delicate. I couldn't see the pregnancy. "Who answered on behalf of Mavis?" I enquired.

In chorus they answered "Antony and Lucia!"

"We don't condone stupidity, Anton and Lucia I'm going to punish you," I fumed. If Mavis was really pregnant, I thought, she had been heavily stigmatized "okay Mavis sit down."

I carried on and finished marking the attendance register. All twenty nine students were present. I instructed Anton and Lucia to thoroughly sweep the classroom soon after lessons. I gave their class monitor Albert Gumpo a task to write down names of noise makers. "You've to read and understand. That's the only way to get something at the end of the year. If you persist making a lot of noise like empty vessels, then it means you're digging your own graves. I only want to hear meaningful noise of constructive discussions"

After making the exhortations, I scurried to form two classes and also admonished them to read and practice. Both form two 'A' and 'B' classrooms were swept clean, I urged them to keep the standard and carry the same spirit to their exercise books for cleanliness is next to Godliness. A new teacher is usually liked so much.

I scuttled back to the staff room. At the reception was a queue of parents paying for their children's school fees, so I didn't converse with Christwish.

"Hie Mr Manyika, you're back … I saw you marking register in form four A' class," said Miss Mombeshora.

"Maybe Mr Chimeri thought I can handle it simultaneously." I said pulling out a chair and sitting down beside her.

"It consumes time for first lessons. It affects either of the classes."

"He said Mr Mupanda will be back in three days' time."

"Okay its better then."

"But it wasn't a noble idea since I don't teach in form fours."

"So you're a little bit lucky, because both form four classes are full of naughty students," she said.

I had an opportunity of telling Miss Mombeshora and Mr Chesa who had just entered into the staff room in search of Mr Zabhura , what transpired when I marked form four A' attendance register, the issue of 'pregnant' Mavis.

"Her love relationship with Diveris the conductor is well known by all and sundry." said Miss Mombeshora.

"I heard Diveris ditched her during the holiday." Mr Chesa pointed out "we're going to sit and counsel her tomorrow morning. She must focus on school work."

"I saw her face, she is in despair!" I chipped in. Diveris the conductor was a guy of loose morals I remembered him very well. Douglas's accomplice! His partner in crime. At Cashel valley bus station where I boarded the bus, I saw him conversing with a harlot. His arms around that whore and they were nearly kissing in public. Her anopheles mosquito's head was shaved the Mohican style, her face ghastly powdered and her eyes were big and lusty. She had a body any woman would kill to have though. It was evident enough to prove that Diveris was of a lewd character, really licentious. I felt pity for the unsuspecting Mavis.

Girl child protection units should be put on at Ward and District levels so that they elucidate issues of child abuse in their awareness campaigns. It bled my heart to see communities degenerating into a sinkhole of debauchery and immorality. A confused generation! The young girls are also in such a dopey emanating from avariciousness.

I spent the rest of the day coping schemes.

Part Two

It was around one o'clock in the afternoon when the pupils were dismissed to go home since it was the first day at school. Usually when schools are still starting, there will be less classes as the teachers will be preparing for a fresh week to start teaching. I overheard some of the students unscrupulously shouting "madam Madziva wore a napkin!" that was a high degree of naughtiness. I was disgusted by that indiscipline and disobedience, but I didn't manage to pinpoint the culprits. It was not good for a student to say such words to a teacher. Actually a napkin is a piece of cloth used at a meal to wipe the fingers or lips and to protect clothes. But the culprits intended to mean nappy' which is a piece of material wrapped around a baby's bottom and between the legs to absorb urine and feaces. It's a common mistake among nursing mothers also. We often hear them saying 'napkins are expensive and laborious because there's need for soap to wash them, so we've resorted to diapers.'

"Today Mrs Madziva wore a see through. I was ashamed on her behalf." Said Shylet.

"She seemed to be unperturbed about her dress." I replied.

"It's not modish, she made a monumental blunder."

"Self-esteem goes away from you with your permission."

"I remember that quote very well. She has fritted away her self-esteem so cheaply."

"It was unmindful of her."

"Her transparent dress nauseated me" she said whilst frowning.

"What are the narcotics causing such unconsciousness as far as fashion is concerned? Because you look! Indecent dressing is now the order of the day."

"I think its lack of ethics. I remember at one point I visited my young sister at a boarding school in Bulawayo. We found the shapely matron sheathed in skin tight slacks, yet supposed to be modest and exemplify moral standards." Miss Mombeshora had chipped in.

"But let's not exonerate the culprits, It was lousy." said Shylet primly staring at Mr Chesa who didn't comment and remained dump aloof.

"There is need for exigent exorcism in these students." I said facetiously.

"She made a big flaw, but did you notice the nappy ..." Miss Mombeshora stopped backbiting Mrs Madziva after noticing her entering the staff room. Surely the dress deserves moral outrage. I averted my eyes, but at the same time burn with curiosity of seeing the said nappy.

Nowadays some moral restrains have been eroded. Values have unethically replaced virtues and in the present highly liberalized societies, people are free and they feel justified in choosing their own values the way they would just choose groceries in a supermarket. In this shame particular case, I don't know why Mrs Madziva preferred or valued such a semitransparent dress, yet there are some teacher ethics with modest and formal dress codes that should've guided her. It seems she lost the dignified dressing ethics and along with it, it's moral compass.

However, she was so friendly, "good afternoon Mr Manyika. I've come looking for you. I've a request." said Mrs Madziva coming towards our table. You know it's no proper to converse with someone whilst looking aside, plus curiosity kills a cat. So I managed to throw some furtive glances at her. She had wrapped an azure cloth primly for the betterment of the situation but visibly she was pregnant.

"What's your request madam?"

"My young sister is going to rewrite English language, June exams. Can you offer her some extra lessons during the weekends? She is lagging behind."

"Okay I'll have to see her first, so that we can arrange."

"Thank you. I think you better come for supper at my place and you'll meet her."

"Okay madam it's all fine with me." I replied.

"Two houses behind yours, the one next to Shylet's."

"At what time?"

"Six o'clock, the sooner the better." she said.

"Okay madam I'll be there by quarter to seven." I whispered ardently and remained phlegmatic. She walked away friendly, smiling brightly and so nice that I felt like following her, which made me realize how dangerous these false appearances can be for society.

Part Three

"Mr Manyika, this is Yolanda my house maid." said Mrs Madziva wrapped in an azure cloth but had changed the previous outrageous dress into a printed silk one.

"How are you Yolanda? It's nice to meet you." I greeted her.

"I'm fine sir. It's nice to meet you too." Yolanda replied shyly. She was a young girl, dark and pale, with thick hair that looked as if it needed a brush.

"My young sister Barbra has just departed for Mayo Chendambuya, if she doesn't proceed to Harare, she'll be back in four days' time. She usually spends most of her time perambulating. But her absence won't stop us having supper together" said Mrs Madziva with a smile on her face.

"But ma'am … there's no enough mealie meal." said Yolanda with a trembling feeling.

"Stupid!"

"I realized it today in the morning ma'am."

Without shy, Mrs Madziva vomited vituperative words to the young girl, words which I can't say. Yolanda started quivering all over and her words would not come freely. She was bare footed and I saw she was now sick with fear of what the future looks like. "Sorry Mr Manyika you'll probably think I'm hysterical, or over melodramatic but I'm not. It's only this moron. She is the one who does cooking everyday but she didn't inform me in time that there is no enough mealie meal."

"Forgive her madam, mistakes are common. She forgot." I said. She smiled in embarrassment maybe after realizing her mistake of donning a semitransparent dress in which she paraded herself the whole day in.

"Yolanda!"

"ma'am"

"Quickly make tea! Manyika is hungry. I think there're enough scones for the three of us." Instructed Mrs Madziva. Yolanda remained rooted, her head dipped and her eyes kept lowered, her eye balls rolling sidewise in fear. "Yolanda! Are you deaf? I said go and make tea! Did you hear what I said?" she asked her harshly whilst shaking the little girl violently, maybe to jar her memory.

"Ma'am … ma'am," the girl's voice died away and tears came to her eyes. Mrs Madziva gave the girl's head a final jerk. "There … there is no shhh sugar ma'am." Yolanda said with the clutch of fear on her throat, staring at the floor and plucking at her apron.

Mrs Madziva stared at her, her lips parted. Suddenly she snuffled, her nose running then blew her nose noisily on her handkerchief and said to Yolanda, "My cold and headache is getting worse. Get me some aspirin." Yolanda went to the bedroom to collect the medicine moving slowly like a mourner approaching bier to view the deceased. "Ugh!" exclaimed Mrs Madziva, "This girl is sleeping on duty!" she looked confused and took her handkerchief again, blew her nose with a tremendous snort, and then clenched her hands in despair.

"Don't worry madam …" I tried to comfort her but she interjected

"No! She is nitwit."

"I think she isn't dimwit, maybe Barbra was aware."

"Both of them are stupid." she said and frowned.

Yolanda came back with the aspirin and a glass of water "ma'am Barbra took all scones …" she paused after we heard a knock on the door. I'm intelligent enough to distinguish between a man and a woman's knock on the door, judging by the sound and frequency. It was a man's knock on the door. My mind quickly wondered about Mrs Madziva's pregnancy. I had never heard about her husband. But I wondered also on the reason why she was residing at the single quarters if she has a husband and a maid.

"Go and see who is knocking on the door."

"Okay ma'am." Yolanda replied and went to open the door.

"Good evening Yola?" It was a familiar voice, but the man refused to enter as Yolanda stepped aside to let him in. "I'm not coming in, I've just bought this coke for Mrs Madziva."

Mrs Madziva blinked with surprise, "ooh! Thank you so much Mr Zabhura, I thought you were lying that you'll buy me a liter. Ooh Christ! This is serendipitous!" she shouted with an excited voice.

"Thank you Sir" said Yolanda.

"I'll come to collect the empty bottle tomorrow. I've to return it to the shop."

"Okay sir."

"Good night all of you."

"Same to you." Yolanda closed the door and came with the bottle. But before she placed it on the table, somehow the one liter coca cola bottle slipped from her hands and fell with a loud explosion on the floor.

There was a grave silence which then engulfed the room. Fortunately my cellphone rang. But for a moment I stared at it like a priest interrupted in the middle of a prayer by the devil. "Hullo good evening Mr Chimeri …" It was just a minute call. The caller didn't give me the chance to reply further for his tone and message was so commanding.

To my host I said, "I've just received a phone call from the headmaster. He wants a copy of my ID immediately. He said tomorrow he will be away at the District Office." I said whilst standing up and henceforth heading towards the door.

CHAPTER 3

Part One

"Today Mr Chimeri is not available. I'm the one in charge!" braggingly said Mr Chesa and pointed out, "let's maintain discipline. Obviously when the cat is away, the mouse will play. Let's show the mice that small cats are as good as the bigger cat." We busted into laughter after being labeled small cats and Headmaster the big one. I was comfortably seated in between two beautiful ladies in the staff room. But there was a hotchpotch of perfumes getting into my nose as usual. "We don't want to waste time, let's start our today's business please! Manyika! Kick the ball rolling." Chesa concluded.

All class teachers had to go and mark attendance registers first before commencement of lessons. I stood up in search of Mrs Madziva but she had gone already. Today she was well dressed in a nice blue ladies suit. She was extremely neat. She looked as if she has just been delivered from the dry cleaners; I had the feeling that if you put out a hand to touch her, you would be prevented by an invisible plastic coating.

I decided to start with form four A' register since it was the most important class. When I entered the classroom, student's voices faded and died altogether as they had been making a lot of noise. All of them were present except the 'pregnant' Mavis, and no one knew her whereabouts. I thought she had fallen sick maybe a headache or a stomachache.

The form one B classroom was swept clean and all of them were present except the one Nadia who eloped during the holiday.

On my way back to the Administration block I met a very tall girl, as tall as a crane, with fair hair cut short. She wore a dress that was a bit too long and too big and she looked slightly dowdy.

"Hey Mary! come back! Let's meet at Deputy Head's office." That was Mr Zabhura calling back the girl. Who is this Mary? Where was she heading to? She seemed she intended to have one or two words with me. "Manyika! Let's meet at Mr Chesa's office." said Zabhura to me.

We crowded round in the Deputy Head's office, the three of us and Mr Chesa, Mrs Madziva and Mrs Mawuru. Senior lady Mrs Mawuru was tall and dignified and almost grey haired. We were standing opposite each other, whilst Mr Chesa and the girl sat on chairs opposite each other over his table. Mrs Mawuru's dark eyes kept staring into Mary as if they would skewer into her soul. She was a woman of about sixty, with a smile she occasionally switched on and off like an electric fridge. "How are you young girl?" greeted Mrs Mawuru, and she switched on the smile, which warmed up nicely; then it switched off and her face went cold again.

"I'm fine mam." replied Mary.

"Who are you? And what brought you here this morning girl?" asked Mr Chesa.

"I'm Mary, Mavis's elder sister"

"Mr Manyika is Mavis present today?" asked Mrs Mawuru.

The tone of her voice gave me a twinge because I remembered Mavis being stigmatized in front of my face. "She is absent today and no one knew her whereabouts." I replied.

"Mary where is Mavis? Let's give her the platform so that she can gasp out her story." said Mr Zabhura.

"Mavis is currently admitted at the clinic, we went with her early morning at around 4am." said Mary with a squeaky voice.

"Ooh she has fallen sick poor Mavy." said Mrs Madziva. Her voice too seemed to have been dry cleaned.

"No she … she … actually she …" Mary's voice faded. She stopped and sobbed.

"Try to collect your strength Mary, and tell us what actually happened." I said.

She nodded and then clenched her hands and seemingly forced herself to continue. "she committed abortion!"

"What!" we exclaimed in unison.

"She aborted yesterday night." she sobbed.

"Ooh Christ!" exclaimed Mrs Mawuru

"She is currently in a very critical condition."

"Any words from the nurse?" enquired Mrs Madziva.

"He said she must immediately be transferred to Mutare Provincial Hospital, but there's no any ambulance to ferry her."

"What can we do now?" blurted Mrs Mawuru showing a great despair. Mr Chesa seemed to be deep in thought as if meditating. There was a faraway look on Mrs Madziva's face too.

"That isn't' the school's business. Here we don't teach children on how to abort neither did we taught her how to easily get pregnant. We admonish abstinence. We're no to blame because of this tragedy. She knows where she got such kind of evil notes. I only thank this girl for coming to notify us on that sad development." said Mr Chesa almost barking.

"I've come also to supplicate for Mr Zabhura's help." said Mary almost sobbing.

"What sort of help young girl?" asked Mr Zabhura

"A help with your car."

"I don't even remember when I last drove my car. Are you aware of the fuel crisis in this country?"

"Please help us please! Please!" Mary pleaded.

"Girl! Fuel pumps are charging exorbitant mark up prices; I can't afford to buy petrol. They've to call an ambulance."

"There're no ambulances, please help us."

"Have you ringed Mutambara mission hospital?"

"Yes they don't have fuel too; they've only one ambulance which they said is currently in bad condition. It can't reach this area too. Please help us please!"

"My dear … if big institutions like hospitals don't have fuel, so where can I get it? My car is not solar or wind powered. It's a petrol engine."

"Where can I get help, Ooh Lord!" cried Mary.

"Try to seek assistance from Mr Ruchiyo a local businessman. Where is your father?" asked Mrs Mawuru with her face in exacerbated despair.

"He is dead drunk at the moment." she replied.

"Even if you get transport to the hospitals these days either you find medical doctors on industrial action or there's no electricity or the essential medications." said Mrs Madziva with a pitying voice.

Mrs Madziva's lamentation at the possibility of situations at hospitals subdued and reminded me of my late elder brother John Manyika who was involved in a tragic accident. It was very unfortunate. He was struck with a car on his way back from a village beer binge. Due to economic hardships and high unemployment, he and others had found solace from the bottom of a beer mug. They were now addicted to the wise waters. The unlicensed Toyota ipsum driver was also intoxicated. It is very perilous to walk alone or drive whilst stupefied by beer. Eye witnesses said my brother was walking in the middle of the road that led from Nhedziwa growth point to Cashel valley police station at around eight o'clock in the evening. The driver of the Toyota ipsum happened to be our clan's son in law. In a state of inebriation he couldn't notice the object ahead of him, only to apply brakes after bumping him off. My brother then sustained a severe head injury. He was ram-shackled and one could visibly see his skull before scarlet of blood engulfed his butchered head. He bled profusely losing gallons of blood. Somehow Muhamba transformed to sobriety and ferried him to a local hospital but there were no any doctors or seasoned nurses at the health institution only to find inexperienced junior nurses running up and down clumsily.

Indignation seized me after receiving a phone call from Pamela my sister informing me about the tragedy that befallen our brother. By that time I was at Hauna, Honde valley working in a Mega Family Choice supermarket as a till operator.

Mary's cellphone rang very loudly to the extent of alerting a battalion of big rats and a certain unique tribe of cockroaches in the office. She answered her call "hallo! Hallo! Halloo! … Eeh … nurse … what's the current condition … tell me please … aah! You said she what? … What!"

Part Two

My Heart nearly jumped into my mouth after the sad news passed through my ears. I was heavily subdued by the untimely death of Mavis. However we decided to proceed with lessons and would go to pay our deepest condolences to Mavis's family in the afternoon.

My first lesson of the day was in form one 'A'. It was a simplest one since they were going to write spellings' and the same in form one 'B'. In both classes only a few had painstaking handwritings and perfect spellings, for the rest it wasn't easy to decipher their writing. Almost three quarters of the class failed 'biscuits' and 'bicycle' spellings. I could not help laughing out loud at *'biskitts'* and *'buyscool'*.

I was also disappointed by the form two, feebly no one scored above the half mark in a comprehension exercise I had given them. But suddenly it dawned on me that these errors, the clumsiness, were the outcome of a great effort prompted by the love of schooling. As usual, there were those who had not written. One of them was Tracy, a form two girl. I had called her to the staff room. In much amazement I invigilated them writing and saw that everyone was busy writing the answers on their exercise books. But some books were missing on marking. First I called Tracy to clarify on the whereabouts of her English exercise book.

Tracy was just a small prettier girl with a naturally swarthy skin and lizard eyes. "Tracy where is your book? I want it for marking!" I barked. But she was as mute as a doll. I piled on some more questions but she just stared fixedly at me. I realized she was just a block of wood in a school uniform. "You thought you've successfully cheated me but in actual sense you're cheating yourself. Give me your work Tracy!" I was almost fuming now.

She remained on mute for some moments and finally she said, "I'm sorry sir … I was not writing"

"So what were you doing Tracy?"

"I was pretending writing" her voice was lame. I don't even know how I strucked her with a wooden stick that was on the table, only to realize after the stick had broken into two pieces. She was on the verge of tears "I'm sorry sir … I left my English books at home" she said in a shakier voice.

"You've come to the field without a hoe or any tool? Don't fool up yourself by napping in such a way. Okay let me give you a piece of paper to write on it and then you'll transfer the work to your exercise book tomorrow."

"I don't have a pen sir."

"What! … What were you holding when you were pretending concentrating on writing?" I asked staring at her quizzically.

"It was an empty barrel sir."

Unable to bear It anymore, I strucked her again on her open palm with a broken piece of the stick and gave her my own black pen. I felt disappointment and frustration well in my heart as the thoughts of her possible future started to swirl in my mind. It was crystal clear that she had a bleak future ahead if she doesn't change. I tried to shake my head to clear it but the myriad of thoughts clung on tenaciously. Out of anger I went to thrash all those who didn't submit their books for marking. I was furious and I spanked boys using a stick. Tears were the only sign I considered I had disciplined the culprits enough.

Part Three

"John Cearner disturbed my Shona lesson in form four B' class. He was behaving like someone possessed with evil spirits, but I think it's due to drug abuse. He was smelling marijuana. When I tried in vain to chase him out of the classroom he shouted something about me being a bitch and other nasty things which I can't repeat. Morgan the janitor came to my rescue and he had a fist fight right in the middle of the classroom. They pommelled each other. The first blow struck Morgan on the head and he went down. He stood up and they struggled again on their feet and they tumbled to the floor. Morgan was eventually overpowered; I think the first blow had done something on his head. So John Cearner managed to pin him on the floor and was sitting on top of him. I could see tears of pain rolling down his cheeks. He was released and JC exited the room after the fight remonstrating that the new teacher Mr Manyika had beaten his form two little sister. Raucously he said, "Manyika should resign immediately or else I'll personally deal with him." the other form four B' students were in full support of him. Right now I think he went home or he is hiding somewhere smoking marijuana. I failed to continue with the lesson, but I saw Morgan busy cutting grass at the grounds which implies he wasn't injured. I thought he also reported the matter to Mr Chesa but I'm aware JC is hard to deal with"

A deathly silence came over the staffroom as the dry cleaned Mrs Madziva finished her story. Even the Deputy Headmaster's face wore a solemn and somber expression. I casted my eyes at Mrs Madziva, she appeared such a frail and tormented soul. I didn't know that ferocious John Cearner but It was clear that the name was just a sobriquet given to him after the famous world wrestling champion. Mr Zabhura bemoaned the incident.

The boy had already besmirched Morgan and Mrs Madziva and I was next, but as a karate black belt holder I wouldn't capitulate. "Mr Chesa! Why don't you expel this so called John Cearner from school?" I asked.

"He is very hard to deal with … his parents too."

Bluntly I asked "why're you so negligent and lenient like that?"

He smiled frankly with malice. He was notably offended by my blunt question. He rubbed a finger along his long nose and said "maybe you're capable of dealing with him young man. Can I call him?" he asked and it was crystal clear that he was further baiting me. I tried to put a smile of my own. "We've to go to Mavis's funeral; you'll probably see him tomorrow morning. I'll give you a gold medal if you manage to chase him. He is the biggest problem at this School. Even local police gave up! Moreover this benighted community supplicated he should come and learn despite his naughtiness." he said.

I wasn't baffled with the sentiments though "but why don't you discuss the issue with the District Educator, because I know it is your wise recommendations that influence the final decisions?"

"Mr Chimeri is still in the process of discussing It with him, this means he has a deal he is still cooking" he paused and then totted, "okay let's prepare to go and bid Mavis a farewell. Mr Manyika! You're going in her class teacher's capacity"

O' Level English language teacher madam Nyagomo had previously requested me to monitor her form four B' English class, but John Cearner was nowhere to be found.

Part Four

We trotted at a lively pace in a narrow dust path that diverted to the east side of the school just after the lemon tree orchard. We were four, the leader of the pack Mr Chesa, Mr Zabhura, Mrs Mawuru and myself. After twenty minutes, we finally arrived at the gravel main road. We caught sight of Morgan among a group of school boys, there seemed to be a desperate gaiety about him. He saw us and waved like a drowning man, but we kept walking.

I noticed Mrs Mawuru was now walking with difficulty. "The responsible authorities are taking people for granted. Can you see! The poor state of his gravel road" pointed Mrs Mawuru.

"Six solid years without maintenance." said Mr Chesa.

"Seven years!" protested Mr Zabhura "The bad part of it is that, people continue to vote for someone who is not productive." he totted.

"Last elections he campaigned and promised to revamp this poor road, but upon re-election, he went AWOL as usual." said Mr Chesa, his face worriedly.

"He'll come back with another bunch of lies prior to the next elections, but you'll be surprised to see him warming the bench again in parliament." said Mr Zabhura.

"Four consecutive terms retaining his seat in parliament!" Cried Mrs Mawuru. She added "we don't have a library because of him. He is busy enjoying squandering CDFs, Community Development Funds. Some of these politicians of his ilk just enjoy chewing that fund forgetting people who elevated them. You know what? Last year he diverted a lorry carrying donated maize seeds to his personal farm. It's not fair!'

I noted that a lot of people are just entering into politics for the love of money and popularity. They don't have the poor people they represent at heart. It needs divine intervention in electing a real and politically mature person to represent them in the National Assembly.

"But why do people continue re-electing such a non-productive greedy, corrupt pot-bellied fellow? ... Do they become blind or sleep the moment they touch the ballot paper?" I asked rhetorically.

"No! They vote for him willingly, still covered by a cloud of euphoria invoked by the goodies he brought for them prior to elections. So it's like one month of enjoying, whistling and ululating and then the rest five solid years crying incessantly in that ordeal." said Mrs Mawuru.

"I recently listened to the radio and heard reports that a Mayor stole maize meant for welfare, it's very disheartening. People continue lionizing corrupt fat creatures who doesn't have them at heart." lamented Mr Zabhura.

"It's like our MP turns off his mobile phone after the elections, only to pop up prior next elections." said Mr Chesa and he pointed out "look at these pot holes in the middle of the road! Deep enough to plant eucalyptus trees"

"They're no longer simple pot holes, they're now water wells!" Protested Mr Zabhura.

"Suitable for fish farming." exaggerated Mrs Mawuru.

I had to ask, "so how are the people surviving?"

"The soil around here is so dry and barren." Mr Zabhura added "fishing helps these people to make a living ..."

"But most of them are practicing it illegally using the prohibited mosquito nets." interjected Mrs Mawuru.

"Here there's a void in any progressive or any developmental projects like irrigation schemes for instance. People are relying on food donations from NGOs. The people are so sloth too, which further qualifies them as perennial candidates for food aid. It's like they're in a delirium evoked by dependency syndrome." said Mr Chesa. I deduced a lot of people are too submissive and sluggard politically. They just drift with the tide. They just follow wind direction at that particular political moment. This shilly-shallying weakness in political destitutes hinders development in their respective constituencies. Some people tend to lionize and hero worship corrupt politicians rather than viewing them as brood of vultures pillaging and smuggling community resources for personal aggrandisement. This knowledge made anger climb up inside me. A disgusting 'me first', look out for number one attitude seems to have become the rule among morally degenerated , ingenuine, inept corrupt politicians who amass wealth and fill their large infinity pockets and those of their close relatives, whilst electorate side-lined.

It's not fair! We've suffered!

Is it because we're sleepwalking as a whole?

Our beautiful country is endowed with a lot of precious minerals but we're languishing in abject poverty. Are we all sleepwalking on top of those worthy stones?

I also loathe the notion of some people politically calling on for the imposition of Trade or Economic embargoes from EU.

Notionally, it's like inborn identical twins fighting intrauterine and one foetus call on for the blockage of the placenta which embodies the trading platform, anticipating its own umbilical cord and amniotic sac in form of international relations and its political party respectively would smoothly remain vigorous. This has hindered economic development. How do we progress? How do we survive? We've all suffered! This country is very rich in minerals, very fertile soils apt for agriculture, wildlife, resorts, tones of both rhino and elephant ivory etc. We deserve bread and butter. Of course we've the ingredients: milk, flour, baking powder, sugar, butter etc. but ironically we're actually sleeping with empty stomachs. Maybe we don't have the stove! But where is the beneficiation issue? Let's awaken as a nation and see where we're wrong footing. Everyone, every citizen must benefit equally from our God given wealth as a nation. Fat cats in form of politicians must cease claiming the lion's share. We've suffered! Few individuals should desist from amassing wealth and enriching themselves at the expense of the generality of the people. To arouse astonishment in slumbering electorate, demagogue corrupt orators are quiescent in welfare and developmental issues.

"Ugh!" Sighed exhausted Mrs Mawuru. The main gravel road had been long and her feet were now dusty. Mr Chesa also dragged his feet like a tired sportsman. We took another dusty path that meandered along Ndyere stream between two valleys. The path was still climbing above terraces of untilled land covered with dry grass.

After twenty minutes we caught sight of a small village perched above us on a hill top. "That's Svinurai village!" Mr Chesa announced.

"I feel pity for our pupils; they come from a very long distance this freezing winter." I said pitifully.

"They're used to walk. It's not a big deal for them. There're four more villages after Svinurai. There's Masori, Mudima, Kamboma and Makuhunga. They all fall under our school's catchment area." replied Mr Zabhura.

Finally we reached the village after passing through Thabanchu Primary School. We caught sight of a house where multitudes of people were gathered outside, singing sorrowful funeral songs. "You see!" Mrs Mawuru cried "a lot of people have been very shocked."

Personally what troubled me more was the thought on how Mavis was stigmatized in my presence, I also noticed certain uneasiness in Mr Chesa.

That funeral, though solemn, had been lively and full of song and dance. The sun was at its zenith and hell hot, it had been a hot long-day. Mavis had breathed her last. A lot of people had come to pay their last respects and bid farewell to her corporal remains. After an hour or so of song and prayer, the Priest announced in anticipation of Mavis's burial the following day. From my vantage point, I could see her mother dressed in black, a sincere sign of her pure grief, as dictated by tradition. Flanking on her right side was Mavis's grandmother and at her left was Mary.

After some minutes we grabbed an opportunity to talk to their neighbour Mrs Chibvuri. "Mavis was really pregnant. Three months pregnant. But her boyfriend Diveris ill advised her to terminate the pregnancy yet abortion is legally wrong and morally unacceptable. Unfortunately it is said Mavy didn't impeccably follow the prescription they got from the witchdoctor Diveris has paid. That led to her untimely death. It's very painful. I can't believe it!" Cried Mrs Chibvuri.

"Where is Diveris?" Mr Chesa enquired. The libertine conductor was not on site.

"He snubbed the funeral. I don't know if he'll come for the burial tomorrow, but I heard his accomplice Douglas is currently in police custody." Mrs Chibvuri paused for effect and pointed out. "Most of those who seat on top of vehicle engines are sexually abusing school girls"

"Are there any police reports made so far? Diveris have a case to answer!"

"No any reports have been made. Also there's a big stumbling block since there's no any vehicle to ferry the body to Mutare General Hospital for post-mortem."

"So what'll happen?"

"The village Head has already sent a green light for burial tomorrow, but still there're squabbles within the family over that decision." said Mrs Chibvuri and added. "Plus they don't have a funeral policy. The funeral could've been well organised and everything run smoothly. But in these folks, joining a funeral policy is highly considered as a taboo."

For sure, advertising funeral policy packages to some people is just as good as selling contraceptives to Catholic nuns. Joining a funeral policy doesn't mean one prematurely dies the moment he or she sign the papers or does it ensure to predicaments and culminate in early mortality. Those who rely mostly in African Traditional Religion might think that their ancestral spirits or spiritual guidance could snub them the moment they give in to westernisation. Of course there are also a lot of dubious and some bogus Policy companies that've sprout like grass in Zimbabwe. One needs to scrupulously scrutinize a company of choice and henceforth join an apt funeral plan that would come in with support as things get tough as far as death is concerned. No one is immortal. Death just happens unexpectedly without ringing warning bells in advance in some instances. Somnambulist fellows do not consider that funeral policies provide the much needed assistance.

I was heartbroken to learn that there was no any sort of organisation at Mavis's funeral. Community funeral groups are also laudable. I've seen them in different communities well organised. All funeral essentials are provided by the group from its savings. Even food is bought from the members small contributions per month, depending on the number of benefactors. There was nothing like that at Svinurai village.

Mavis's family had a splitting headache on where to find a coffin since the local carpenters were placing high prices on that wooden box prior to be eaten by termites at six feet underground.

There were also boiling tensions between the family members on whether to bury the deceased without compensation from Diveris or not. I observed it was a tornado of a squabble between African Traditional Religion versus Christianity. The latter group were lenient and forgiving, citing various complications that would possibly arise if they decide to keep the dead body. They also pointed out Diveris's family hinting that Mavis was not dragged to a witchdoctor but she personally weighed, whether she used an analogue or a digital, whatever the scale she found worthy and admitted the idea of abortion despite the adverse consequences. Moreover they hinted that the witchdoctor didn't spoon fed her but she took the unspecified herbs willingly. Dead is dead, burying her was ideal and henceforth solve other issues thereafter burial.

The former group was adamant also citing various vital reasons. I personally overhead one of the family elders from the ATR faction saying "it's very crucial to summon him and his family elders first; then we solve our differences amicably. In my modest opinion they've to assist us with other things needed at this funeral. After burial we sit for a meeting and charge them beasts that commensurate with the degree of the offence. Diveris shouldn't go Scot free; otherwise our ancestors will get angered and wipe all of us including the small innocents, thus the lethal part of it!"

One of the white bearded elders interjected, "let's charge them before burial! We only bury the corpse after settling the matters. If we don't reach consensus we can give them the deceased!" He pointed out frighteningly,

"Mavis will wake up a ghost if we don't properly handle this case! That is that!" He barked.

In my own point of view, a boiling Vendetta to culminate in litigations was imminent. The African Traditional Religion faction was gaining ground despite their own differences traditionally to the frustration of Christians.

Somehow, serendipitously Amon the Headman arrived in time to extinguish the flames. I heard he was one man respected by everyone in the community. He was aged between seventy two and seventy four, but I was surprised to hear villagers calling the septuagenarian by his first name, nevertheless, ironically they showed him respect. He wasn't offended by that, but actually he enjoyed being called by his first name. He was a very short man, as short as the word 'short' itself. Amon was simulacrum to the biblical Zacchaeus. His head was aptly decorated with grey hair which is also biblically likened to a crown. He was humorously goat bearded. There was anticipated tranquillity upon his arrival which implied that he had already quenched the inferno successfully with his mere arrival.

After ten minutes of exchanging words in whispers with the family elders from both factions, he stood up to make announcements but he was too short to be seen. He then opted to stand on top of a table at the front. I was amused by what I considered a comedy but all other mourners didn't laugh at it. It implies that they were now accustomed to seeing him finding artificial means to increase his height just like the biblical Zacchaeus who climbed on a tree to amply converse with Jesus Christ. "I've intervened as the Headman!" Braggingly shouted Amon. "We're all sad." he pointed out "there was a stiff disagreement here! But I've managed to find a suitable Panacea to it. I've a very big tank of solutions. I'm short but not short of ideas!" He fetched a laugh up from his guts but in despair and paused to wipe a sweat-beaded forehead. "Right! We're going to bury Mavis our daughter tomorrow. We've summoned everyone who has to be summoned. Let's put all our hands together and help this family because I don't think they can handle it themselves. As the elders we're solving the issue in utmost good faith. You also know there is the issue of spirits and ghosts. The primitive fear of the dead is strong within some of us, but let me assure you that Mavis's death doesn't mean she's now an enemy. The dead do come back yes, but it's not always that they mean us harm." Amon's voice was well cultured.

One of the Christian elders, previously introduced as Pastor Elias Mashoko was seated behind us, with a very low voice he mumbled "a dead person is dead, there's no such things as ghosts. Yes there are evil spirits unleashed from the devil trying to confuse people. Why fearing the dead? Of course Diveris have to be summoned. But dead is dead till resurrection. This has made anger bubble inside me, these people are in pitch darkness, not yet enlightened." He then bursted into a low provocative laughter that later died somewhere in his throat as mysteriously as it had started.

CHAPTER 4

Part one

On Thursday, the illuminous bright sun rose above the horizon of Mandima. It illuminated Oxford Secondary School, fretted to the north by the purple shadows of Guhune Mountains.

I had finished my morning lessons, and now seated in the staffroom busy marking children's work at around half past ten in the morning. The Head had earlier on hinted on the possibility of releasing all children to attend Mavis's burial. "We're now ringing the bell; all students are going to attend her burial. But for you teachers, it's optional since you've a lot of work." said Mr Zabhura.

I wasn't scandalised by that decision since Oxford Secondary was a small School, Mavis was well known by all and sundry. I decided not to turn up for burial, so I remained alone in the staffroom. I felt very lonely for up to twenty five minutes until I heard a sweet mellifluous voice calling on me. "Samanyikaaa!"

I looked back and saw a shapely silhouette against the light from the window. I couldn't help noticing that her voice had a rich vein of musicality. I also noticed for the second time that she had the perfect eyes to match the sweet voice. She lowered her bulk body on to a chair. "Ooh I forgot my cell-phone at the reception, let me go and collect it. Ooh Christ! My cellphone is my baby." she cried and carried herself well, with her head high on her long beautiful neck, so that she looked taller than she was.

Christwish had an unhurried, dignified walk though. I observed she wore a wig. Anger started to boil up in me, but it was anger that had no serious target. I wasn't angry with Christwish or any teacher or the students. But I think it was because of those who manufacture wigs. It was the sort of anger that suddenly attacks a man when he finds himself in a situation he can't control.

She came back, stopped in the middle of the staffroom, turned and faced me. Somehow her wig fell down to the floor as she tried to bent picking up magazines that were on a chair. She couldn't help laughing out loud, I also laughed, a loud bark. "Sorry for yourself." I said

"Well, it's a woman's burden." she smiled at herself, trying to keep her courage up.

"But your natural hair is beautiful." I complemented and she blushed. She was fortuitous I was the only witness.

I hid my feelings as best as I could. Christwish donned the wig again but this time mischievously like a beret. She was now unconcerned about it. "This wig is very beautiful, isn't it?" She enquired.

"Yes it is." I replied.

She grinned more broadly, now as unabashed as ever at being found out in a false look. "Tonde my boyfriend bought it on valentine's day in a posh boutique somewhere in Borrowdale. It coated him, Christ knows how much. But I like it very much and I look more beautiful when I'm in it, but naturally I'm good looking. It's only because of him." she said whilst leafing through a copy of The Edgar's Fashion magazine. There was nothing to say but only to nod in agreement, you don't get anywhere disagreeing with a woman's assessment of herself. Of course she was really good looking but I happened to loathe the artificial thing. "You're looking dejected Mr Manyika! Have you eaten something? Usually male bachelors don't cook often."

"I'm fine dear, not hungry. I devoured bread and peanut butter."

She looked at me critically, then shook her head and said, "you've to cook Mr Manyika, won't you?" Her concern for me was touching. In return I smiled at her. Christwish tend to help me in a higher regard than I deserved. She blinked and said, "Ooh I heard that very long ago, our ancestors Manyika and Miranda were good friends."

"Then we've to rekindle that great friendship. But Christwish, now isn't the time to be digging up ancient history." I said. I smiled and suddenly she smiled too. Her smile was remarkably beautiful; it actually lit up the whole of her face. It wasn't just an expression of white teeth.

"You're afraid of John Cearner, aren't you?" Abruptly she asked.

A man doesn't like being asked such a question by a woman. "I'll thrash John Cearner, I'll teach him a lesson to remember."

She must have seen the doubt clearly mirrored on my face for she smiled mysteriously. "But he's very hard to deal with, he is really devilish, so be careful with him. He might also unleash his gang."

Intrepidly, "I'm a soldier enough to turn this School into a military academy. But where did this intractable John Cearner came from?"

"He was transferred from Nyahondo High School after slapping the Headmaster. Mr Ngwende the teacher who wrote his transfer letter cited that 'he is a thug; you might take him at your own risk'. I don't know why our School accepted him. He has repeated O'level thrice, but he's not repenting. His devilry behaviour is increasingly unbecoming." she said.

"I personally happen to remember Nyahondo High School Head, Mr Masimura, a big man, all bone and muscle. At times he looked too big for his shirts."

"I also knew him very well; Rachel my young sister was once at Nyahondo before she transferred to Mutoko. Despite his outward appearance, underneath is a simple man who believes in educational principles and the desire to instill the best education and behaviour in children." Christwish added, hinting: "Maybe our SDC thought JC could transform into a better pupil under Mr Chimeri, but his delinquency has deformed and defamed our School's reputation. He has also degraded his guileless classmates. Right now most of them aren't even focused on School work, yet they're the exam class."

"Yes I observed it; most of our students are just as good as bags of manure on top of a bus carrier. They don't know where they're coming from and where they're bound to. It's pathetic!" I said.

"What about the junior classes, are they active in your English language lessons Mr Manyika?" She asked.

"It's very pathetic! ... They're such an idiotic ilk some of them, that when asked what time do they love most at School, they single out lunch time. In lessons they're as mute as dolls. I don't allow them to speak in Shona during my English lessons. I sometimes wonder if I'm running a funeral Parlour. You only notice the high level of exuberance when they're extricated going for break, lunch or sports." I replied.

"Classrooms are more of a sanatorium during English language lessons except Shona." she pointed out. "It's more like teaching blocks of wood in School uniforms."

"I feel pity for our final exam classes, they're so lackadaisical, they'll abruptly awaken towards final exam and start reading maladroit whilst clinched by exam phobia." I sighed and continued. "Yesterday before we went to the funeral, Mrs Nyagomo requested me to monitor her form Four B' English class; she was busy with some work from the District."

"How was the class?" Christwish enquired curiously.

"Poor! I presented them with a litmus test on their oral use of English."

"What d'you mean Mr Manyika?"

"After reading a certain passage, I requested some of them to orally give a summary of the story. The summaries were full of Eeehhh, Eeehhh Eeehhh ..."

Christwish interjected "Eeehhh is our all-purpose gap-filler, neither dissent nor assent ... Yes! Some of us we don't flow, but when you hear someone speaking always filling gaps, it becomes monotonous and disgusting."

"Their nebulous summaries were more of gap fillings, I couldn't bear the mumbo-jumbo"

"It's very pathetic!" Cried Christwish.

"I think the past teacher strikes, demanding a salary increment have adversely affected so many potential students."

"Yes, these students were not learning. They used to come to School minds focused on playing. It's like they have a frisky hangover. Industrial actions have vile effects on students, even in hospitals that's the time when a lot of patients pass away unattended." she lamented.

"The government should make ways to avoid stay-aways, teachers must be well catered for. If the education system downs its tools, the results are these lethargic students to ripe nothing but a chain of Us'

"Us! They euphemistically call them cups." she giggled.

It's true, some students end up getting cups in lieu of ladders, as a result of a strike aftermath. Those who press the refresh button, ruefully start creeping back to form three. It seems when peaceful salary upward review negotiations between Teacher Unions and the Government hit a snag, strikes are the only way they use in order to be heard and their grievances to be addressed. But the strikes possess negative consequences to both students and their parents, and in the long run the whole nation at large.

Students are short-sighted drowsy walkers who constantly need guides for them to progress and succeed in their educational attainment. In that gloomy atmosphere, learning is disrupted. Time lost can never be recovered. It requires a student's individual endeavours in order to stay awake and subjugate strike or indolent teacher's negative associated effects. Sporadically some teachers only make cameo appearances to lessons, leaving students very thirsty and unsatisfied.

In some Schools, it's during teacher strikes when students get involved and behove in substance abuse. Some School girls start lingering around public places presenting themselves to molesters.

When the strikes come to halt, students are taught in rocket speeds to complete syllabuses. The same applies to college and University students and Lecturer strikes leading to adverse labour market effects. The labour market is presented with half-baked professionals. There are some notable years when the international Labour market rejected inimical graduates from our local universities due to the fact that they spent lots of time striking. I remember those years around 2008 when Uncle Nathan returned back home crestfallen and dishonoured. He was called for an interview in Canada. Once he got there, he was in a hell of a situation! Since Science offer the best prospects, Uncle Nathan chose to study Electronic Engineering at a local University. But the duration of the course was characterised with a lot of strikes by both students and their Lecturers. Students were fulminating against high tuition and accommodation fees yet very low standards provided in return. On the other side, their mentors protested against a peanut salary. Noteworthy is the fact that some of the protests were also politically motivated and led to learning disruptions.

Ironically those years, local universities pumped more degrees than Muammar Gaddafi's Lybia pumped crude oil.

Uncle Nathan went to Canada, his head high. Unfortunately he failed some electronic engineering questions that were considered basic. Instantly, he was told they made a blunder by calling him yet they were aware of incessant strikes that swallowed the larger part of the year he graduated.

University fiascos has led to the increase in the likelihood of being unemployed. That unemployment has turned some inimical graduates into

Street vendors. He had had to cope with the stress and shame of returning back home, yet he left his mother basking in reflected glory propagating the news of her son's success. He is now a well-known radio and television further circuit damager near Tsanzaguru bus terminus in Rusape.

Lecturer strikes are evil! I'm telling you. Even those MCHMB guys were affected and churned out incomplete. I mean those inimical medical doctors who graduated during University strikes. I once heard of a small girl consigned to be placed in the mortuary before she had actually died. Fortuitous enough, she managed to come back to the land of the living just as the nurses were carrying her corpse into the freezer. In a flight, one of them had to permanently break a leg in an attempt to escape from the ghost and was not the only casualty.

Yawning wearily, Christwish said in a voice that was husky with sleep; "I'm tired, I slept today early morning at around one o'clock." Surreptitiously peeping at her watch, she made a movement of being about to get up.

"What? ... Ooh okay I guess you were reading. Are you on block release?" I asked curiously.

"No, not at all. It's only that I love literature."

"What kind of a book? I can see that you were enjoying it"

"I was reading 'Merchant of Venice' by William Shakespeare."

"Okay that one! Shakespeare was a great author."

"Yes, I also borrowed another one called 'Measure for Measure' from Mrs Madziva, but I'm yet to start reading it ..." She paused after we heard some footsteps.

"Mrs Madziva you're here! I thought you went to the funeral!" I exclaimed.

"Ooh no my dear. Can't you see that I'm a double-decker?"

"What d'you mean madam?"

"I'm pregnant; I can't walk to such a very long distance"

"I get it." said Christwish, her voice still husky with sleep.

"I'm looking for some money ... Money to buy fruits, I love fancy apples." Said Mrs Madziva. I opened my wallet and gave her some cash. She appreciated and turned to Christwish, "how was that novel 'Merchant of Venice'?"

"It was exciting, Mrs Madziva."

"I hope Mr Manyika will not demand a 'pound of flesh' if I fail to give him back his money."

We all bursted into a laughter, "If you give birth to a girl, then I'll be your son in law." I said jocundly.

"I'm carrying a baby boy. I went for a scan." she said.

"I love babies especially boys. I don't know why Mavis acted in such a demoniacal way." said Christwish.

"Mavis was a dunce. She could've consulted us. It wasn't that hard to map her way forward in educational attainment. She made a monumental blunder ... As for myself I'm already preparing for my baby boy. I'm even planning in anticipation for his brighter future ahead." said Mrs Madziva, hands clasped across her protruding stomach.

"Where is his father?" Asked Christwish.

"I didn't told you Christwish!" Exclaimed Mrs Madziva and she cooled down. "I thought I told you. You never heard about him?"

"I know nothing about your husband Mrs Madziva."

"Well, he passed away five months ago!"

"He died!"

"Yes he is currently six feet down."

"What happened Mrs Madziva?" I asked.

"It was pneumonia."

"I'm so sorry madam." said Christwish, holding her chin in her hand, with her brows slightly furrowed.

"I sympathise with you madam." I had to ask "what was his name?"

"Bwemba." she replied and added. "he was a well-known senior butcher man at Mega Market."

I knew Mega Market. I once worked for Mega Family Choice and they were our suppliers. She totted, "he was chronically ill."

For a moment Christwish said nothing. Then respectfully: "I'm so sorry for your loss madam. I went on a leave five months ago; maybe that's why I didn't hear about your husband's death. It's so sad."

Mrs Madziva's face was stony at that moment. "It's very unfortunate, his last days on earth were characterised with a lot of strikes in the health delivery system. His reliable doctor was also included in that bandwagon. So my husband couldn't get the essential treatment to keep him alive. After a long struggle battling with a severe pneumonia, on a fateful day during that strike, a student nurse finished him off by erroneously placing him on wrong medication."

"You mean he died due to an error committed by a student nurse!" Cried Christwish.

"Yes, you know that strikes by both seasoned nurses and doctors compromise the standards because of inept relief student nurses. There's high risk of mortality in hospitals due to inadequate care."

I had to ask, "Can nurses and doctors ethically embark on a strike?"

Christwish also added, "such an action undermines the rights of patients."

"Mrs Madziva had to answer, "Doctors and nurses were earning a meagre salary that didn't match their professions, so they were compelled to action! But patient jeopardy is very high during a strike, yet they say it's worth it for some gains they anticipate will receive as a solution."

"That means we've undedicated people in our health delivery system." I blurted.

"They're dedicated and proficient but they feel unappreciated. It's just the same with us Educationalist."

For sure there's a very low quality of patient care during a strike until pay increment issue resolved. Most severely ill people are prone to die. However, the patients can't retaliate by openly lambasting medical practitioners since they're fully aware of the prize. The expression that 'those who reside in glass houses shouldn't throw stones' applies in like situations. Some patients only grumble their grievances whilst in queues at health care facilities. "The government should make avenues to avoid labour issues." I said

"There's plenty of blame to lay. My spouse died just after an hour of taking wrong medication placed on him." cried Mrs Madziva emotionally.

"What happened to the student nurse?"

"She's currently on suspension. The Hospital authorities said they're thoroughly investigating the case before making the indictment. But it's now five solid months, we haven't heard anything yet." she said with a look of affected hurt.

Strikes throw the patient's health at stake.

I was also a victim of a vicious Nurse strike when I was eight. I was attacked by severe malaria. The clinicians were embarking on an industrial action. Since patients are populous during strikes, we went to a local clinic for three consecutive days unattended. I could've died of malaria at the age of eight, if it wasn't the treatment I got from Sekuru Shonhiwa. My father took me to Rusape to seek help from a knowledgeable Herbalist known as Sekuru Shonhiwa. His place in Vengere where he resided was overcrowded the first day we arrived. So my father knocked at the house of a neighbour who owned a closed garage. People were neighbourly in those hard times; the man gave us a place to sleep inside his garage and provided us with food and blankets. I was attended the following mid-day. Sekuru Shonhiwa made concoct of herbs that were potent enough to raise a dead man, and he charged an insurmountable amount of money. My father had to pay in instalments over a period of six months. Fortunately I recuperated and regained my vigour.

By that time, I had a close friend of mine called Brighton. He was asthmatic. When we came back from the Herbalist I was dumfounded after receiving sad news of his untimely departure at the age of nine. It's said; he breathed his last whilst on a clinic patients queue. I was melancholically depressed. My friend and I were very bright at School. Mrs Choto our grade two teacher couldn't pay a lot of attention on us because we could read fluently, without any difficulty unlike our little classmates.

Taking a quick errand back to those childish days of ours, I still remember vividly two days before we both felt sick. We were caught by a furious downpour on our way back from School. There were a lot of shelters to hide but we were very stubborn. When we reached at Brighton's home, we found a huge fire crackling in the fire place. Our School uniforms were drenched. In a tick we were standing naked in front of the fire to our bashfulness. Brighton's mother was expectantly pregnant. His sister grabbed him and rubbed him with a big towel, turning him round and round as if he were an inanimate object. After Brighton, she applied the same treatment to me, and then I was dressed warmly in his clothes. After the rain, his sister accompanied me to our house, where I was heavily berated by my mother.

Unfortunately my friend passed away when his mother was in labour and later in the day gave birth to a bouncing baby girl. It's very disheartening that she gave birth whilst nurses were on a strike, after all he didn't see his new sibling.

However, by that time the government made appropriate measures for the restoration of normalcy in the health delivery system.

I looked back at Mrs Madziva, and somehow sensed she had been watching at me all the time. "Is everything okay Mr Manyika?" She asked anxiety tingeing her voice.

"I'm very fine madam. It's only that at one point when I grew up I was a victim of a nurse strike and I also lost a closest friend of mine."

"Although children seldom know real friendship, as they change friends the way they change School benches, the fact that you still remember him proves that he was a real friendship indeed." said Mrs Madziva and turned to Christwish. "I want you to accompany me to the grocery shops. I can't walk alone. I need someone to chat with along the way."

"I'm very tired madam Madziva, I slept too late." she refused with a voice heavy and husky with sleep.

"It's okay ..." She paused for a moment then. "Mr Manyika can you?"

I replied, "yes I can!"

"Samanyika can bear you good company." said Christwish yawning, stretching her arms above her head.

Part Three

We trotted on a steady pace in comradely silence.

"I thought you could've done better by sending Yola, but I'm now realising this walk is salubrious since it is an exercise itself." I said.

"Walking is the healthiest sport of all. Nevertheless you're still talking about Yola! That day dreaming dunce! I fired her!" Barked Mrs Madziva.

"Was she inimical?"

"She wasn't helpful, she did things tardily. I stayed with her at my own cost."

The upper half of a hot and big sun peered at us from the crest of the hills. She said, "Someone stole my sun hat yesterday, I suspect these pilfering students"

"Yeah, they might be students because every day there're several reports of theft among themselves in classes."

"They begin by pilferage of pens and books then graduate into serious crimes. I don't tolerate such cases, I thrash thieves. That's the way of impeding them behove into notorious criminals" she pointed out, "morals are being thrown out of the window!"

"What d'you mean madam?"

"People are now committing very despicable crimes; they no longer fear or respect the dead. It happened at my husband funeral."

"Are you referring to the wrong medication issue? ... It is said in South Africa there's a medical doctor arrested on allegations of stealing body parts from corpses during post-mortems. That's the highest degree of theft I've ever heard. You're right! Criminals no longer sacredly have respect towards the dead. Thus moral decadence!"

"That case of a medical doctor is too much. Let me tell you the story Manyika ..." She paused whilst patting her head and continued, "we bought a tombstone for my husband's grave, but less than a week after installing the headstone at a cemetery in Gokwe, the tombstone vanished. The grave was left violated. This degree of theft I think has emanated from too much greed and lack of God's fear. I immediately reported the case to the police, but they couldn't trace the culprits. His elder brother went to seek spiritual help from a witchdoctor who then saw four thieves from a spiritual realm, creeping into the cemetery during the darkest hours of the night and in a trice striped the grave. They carried the stone for a distance of about one hundred meters where they had parked their car. They drove off to Harare where they refined it for resale."

"Why are people acting in such ghoulish acts? So you mean some people unsuspectingly buy second hand tombstones! Those that belongs to someone dead!"

"It's currently happening! The thieves can also clean cut it and manufacture kitchen tops, countertops or other things."

"People should consider where to buy things and avoid Street corners. What happened to the thieves?"

"It's said for the first time they decided to replace it with an undervalued one secretly because the deceased himself haunted them. Along the way from Harare the replacement tombstone mysteriously turned into a wooden board of the same size of the stone. On the second time they successfully went with a high valued replacement and furtively placed it on the grave, but they all perished in lethal car accident on their way back to Harare. A mysterious owl sent by the witchdoctor interrupted the driver and he failed to negotiate a curve. They were all mashed as the car rolled for several times. It was difficult to tell who is who!"

"The witchdoctor went an extra mile!"

"He could've just identified them and left the case for the Police and culprits brought to book."

Surely 'five finger discount' habits shouldn't be condoned starting at the roots, at an early age of stealing sugar or peanut butter at home. Children must be taught to harness only good habits. One's conscience must be serviced and in good condition, ringing warning bells whenever temptations arise.

Thieves must desist from the immoral act for their own good cause too. I vividly remember very well an incident during my tenure at Mega Family Choice Supermarket at Hauna branch where I worked as a Shop supervisor after being elevated from being a till operator.

There was a swarthy guy called George. I don't know where Gunze found him and the reason why he employed such a dark horse. He never talked about himself; I suspected he had a past. Sometimes he could come to work looking like an orphaned puppy. He worked at the parcel counter. George was a silent killer in terms of 'five finger discount'. Heaven knows where he got the audacity and tactics of searching parcels of unsuspecting customers. He siphoned a lot of cash from people's bags at the parcel counter. No one knows about his shenanigans until the bag issue.

There was a black bag that came with an unknown drunken Omnibus driver from Mutare after work. The security guard of the premises owned by Masere who was on night shift was a dullard. At one point I castigated his laxity. He was called Nyamajo. He just took the bag from the drunkard and placed it on the parcel counter without questioning about the owner of the bag and its contents. On the following day in the morning George saw the bag and enquired about its owner but Nyamajo professed ignorance, only what he knew was that the bag came from Mutare destined for Mega Family Choice. The bag took four days on the parcel counter whilst Nyamajo embarking on a scrupulous search for the driver but with no avail.

Earlier in that same week there was a circulating story of a human head discovered in an idle satchel at Sagambe bus terminus. So no one attempted to dire open the bag due to fear of discovering frightful bizarre things. A wave of relief swept us on the fifth day when Godfrey Chapura who was also a shop supervisor but stationed at Mutare downtown branch came looking for the bag. The bag belonged to his young brother Jonzo. He told us they sent the bag from Mutare after knocking off some beers. They considered the bag a big disturbance since they itched to go dancing in Mandisa club. Unfortunately the driver didn't mention the Chapuras when he handed it to Nyamajo.

One day after a solid month from the day when Godfrey collected the bag, George came to work smarter than ever! He wore a nice pair of blue jeans and an original blue Chelsea football club Jersey. We all gave him some complements for the fashion. Even Mr Gunze a goat bearded, short Zacchaeus, company branch manager exemplified him as someone with brains. Actually buying clothes is one exhibit that've to be done to show one is employed. Other co-workers even went an extra mile of enviously enquiring on how much he bought the nice blue Jersey, but the price he said to have purchased it didn't match his salary. Some swift arithmetic also told me it wasn't possible after deducting rent, food etc. I came to a conclusion that someone a lavish relative gave him.

The morning progressed very well until midday when Jonzo passes-by the shop. He stood by the parcel counter for some minutes. I thought George could feel Jonzo's eyes boring him, but he didn't know him though. They hardly conversed. Then I saw Jonzo now talking to Mr Gunze, after some moments I heard Gunze calling on me to arrange for someone, a temporary relief to the parcel counter. In a trice I assigned this girl Precious to replace George. Mr Gunze and George walked into the office, with the former a step or two behind the latter, like a warder whose prisoner has nearly got away. Jonzo and I also got into the office. George tried to tug away from Gunze but I thwarted him with a thunderous slap and he blurted out all his theft cases. Actually he revealed unburdening some horror and the shock. He went on staring up at the ceiling; he still had one foot in jail.

"I also missed a towel and a used toothbrush that was at the back pocket. At first I suspected the driver, but it's this idiot!" Jonzo barked.

"Where's Jonzo's towel and toothbrush?" Asked Mr Gunze

"I don't know ... I only admired the Jersey." replied George whilst fidgeting or vibrating like a running engine.

"There's such a thing as a pathological liar. Aren't you the one?" I asked whilst making such a movement like about to top him up with another vicious slap. He admitted to have stolen the things. Jonzo made the intention to take off the Jersey from him. They scuffled him while I sat there eyeing them up and down like a mother cat licking it's kitten. Finally Gunze intervened and telephoned Charamba the Director of the company who then dismissed George without pay due to his theft charges. Jonzo took George's smartphone as compensation for the stolen things. But what irked lots of people was George's decision to come to the workplace unscrupulously donning a stolen Jersey where he committed the offence. After some days his wife came inquest for clarification of her husband's dismissal and she later divulged that he committed a similar offence when he was a boy. He stole a friend's underwear! It was discovered when they went for swimming at Ruda River.

Suddenly Mrs Madziva said, "the municipal workers are also involved in theft cases perpetrated at cemeteries."

"Tombstone thefts on graves ignites another grieve in the affected families. People are committing serious crimes. It starts by pilfering when one in childhood days, once conscience is damaged it becomes a big problem. That's where the so called John Cearner has headed." I said

"JC is a very big problem. We're going to end up hiring the army to chase him."

"Don't worry I'll deal with him accordingly."

"His sister is a big thief! But a simple nice looking person. Do you know of such criminal offences committed by simple soft people? You can't suspect them!"

"Yes I know. There was a swarthy parcel counter guy who used to siphon things from unsuspecting customers at Mega Family Choice, but one day his misdeeds surfaced. Lots of people came claiming for their stolen items but he was already fired."

"I also heard about John Cearner's sister, also such kind of a criminal. She was a pathological Thief. I haven't met her but I heard about her stories." she said.

"Share with me what you heard." I was curious.

"She was very bright at School and she proceeded to Tertiary and attained HND in Accounts from Mutare Polytechnic. My husband knew her because after college, Mega Market employed her. She was the one responsible of making out the pay envelopes, because by that time they were paid in hard cash. It was her job too to put the wages in those envelopes after NSSA deductions and so on." she stopped. The wind started whipping at her skirt. We walked along in brief silence listening to our feet crunching over the pathway. Her voice sounded nettled, "all right." she smoothed her hair and made a few silly remarks about the wind and continued, "Her name is Sophia." she pointed out, "she was a serial thief" she paused, then abruptly "she was just as cool the way you're!"

I looked at her quickly, the way you turn and look at someone who's leaned on you, suggestively in a bus. "She bought Typek plain bond papers and cut them into small pieces." she stopped as the wind started whipping at her skirt again. It was a windy day and tree leaves were blowing along the path.

Madam Madziva continued, "a day before the pay date, she went with the slips of paper in her handbag. When the senior Accountant Moses Chieza got the money from the bank, Sophia began her evil works. There was none to watch her in her office since her colleague, um this guy Ronald Mahanyana was on leave. She took the envelopes, opened her bag and took out slips of paper and put them in the pay envelopes. The real money went into the pockets of her bag. It is said the envelopes were neatly stacked inside the strongbox. It was a shocking haul! She embezzled and vanished! The industrial workers were handed their envelopes after work on the following day ... When people are given their wages inside envelopes; they're supposed to cross check instantly! But for my husband and his close friend Mashaya and the rest, their somnolence led to hell of situations. They lingered in town with unopened envelopes in their pockets. It wasn't possible to suspect and to tell which was which by the feel of the fat envelopes." she stopped whilst patting her head and then continued after sighing. It had been a long walk. "Mashaya got into a TM supermarket, that one along Herbert Chitepo Street in Mutare, he requested for help and was given two young ladies to assist and push his groaning trollies full of groceries. There were very long queues at Cashpoints to his rage. He shouted and lambasted the shop management for employing tortoise slow till operators. Upon observing his trollies full of worthy groceries, the Shop manager opened another Cashpoint and Mashaya was served first. He opened a cold soft drink and gulped it down his throat in few seconds, maybe his rage made him sweat and thirsty. His father in law also happened to be in the supermarket with a basket occupied by only one miserable packet of sugar. Upon realising his son in law's fat pocket he humbly accepted a drink not yet paid but offered by Mashaya. He comfortably sipped decorously and let his eyes travel round whilst quenching his thirsty slowly but sure. He was proud of his son in law. Whilst the till operator punched and scanned the items into the billing computer, Mashaya opened another drink, now standing leaning on the counter nursing a weeping-cold soft drink. He was told of the total bill and added some few items. Other shop assistants busied themselves nicely packing the groceries for the big customer whilst other customers envied the man. For sure Mashaya had a fat envelope, he hold a higher position at work, superior to Bwemba. After the billing, he chiefly dipped his hand into his pocket and blazonly forked out a fat brown envelope. His name notably inscribed on the envelope, he opened it whilst piercing low mellifluous whistles looking sidewise ... Abruptly he stopped, took a moment scrutinizing the contents, his face stiffened ... And he fainted!"

We both bursted into a laugh, and I asked her "tell me about your husband, what transpired?" I enquired very curiously.

"Okay I'll tell you on our way back home."

Part Four

We arrived at the shops in the nick of time before they closed.

There were four shops but only two were functioning. The first and bigger one was Ruchiyo General Dealer. It was fully packed. It had two apartments, one for groceries and the other one a hardware. It was crystal clear that the business was running smoothly for the proprietor. I was fortuitous enough to see him. He was seated in a chair just by the exit door, nursing a glass of whisky. I didn't like his face though. It was frightening and was deviantly one eyed.

The air in the shop was hot and thick with a huge crowd of customers queuing at the counter. Mrs Madziva enquired on prices of some items and we exited the shop heading to the next one.

It was called Chikopa Investments, but more of a small tuck-shop. The small shop sold nothing but few basic necessities. Luckily enough, fruits were available. Most of the shelves were occupied by nothing but air. She bought some apples but before we exited, we were caught by a surprise.

There were two grimacing little creatures piping cries on a bench, nicely wrapped in yellow shawls. After a long scrutiny of the two, we concluded they were twins. Before we asked anything, the small girl who happened to be the shopkeeper screamed, "their mother dumped them at that bench!"

Instinctively I shivered and shrugged.

"Shut up idiot!" Shouted an emotionally charged man mysteriously coming from the back of the counter. He came to the bench, standing, with his arms akimbo in front of the babies, he blurted, "Sandra! Why could she abandon these one week olds?" He cried in despair. His jaws were restlessly working on a piece of chewing gum in frustration and his eyes were soaked with tears. He took a hopping step towards the open door and looked up in the sky. "Ooh!" He exclaimed with raised eye brows.

"What's wrong Mr Chikopa? Whose babies are these?" Mrs Madziva asked him anxiously.

With a puzzled face the man replied, "they're mine!"

"Where's the mother?"

"She abandoned them and vanished!"

"How could Mrs Chikopa do such an ungodly thing? I regard her as the most distinguished woman."

He hesitated, as if debating how much he should tell us, "Sandy is the mother of these twins ... Ooh!" He cried.

For a moment Mrs Madziva was dump with surprise. It was crystal clear that Mr Chikopa had been bigamous and drowsily indulging into extra marital affairs with the one Sandra. I saw in his eyes a great tormenting pain and despair. "Who's this Sandra you're talking of?" She asked

"That extraordinarily beautiful girl who dwells at Vhiky. I've now realised she's not a dove but a viper! She was just after my finances. She made me chase my wife ... Oh ooh!" He remorsefully cried and totted, "I blame myself, getting myself involved with her in the first place. I let her spoil my marriage. Formerly I had a decent marriage, with a wife I could talk to and kids" he lamented ruefully.

"What transpired in the first place that led to the abandonment? I can see these babies have a febrile of a very serious fever." she said whilst examining one of them.

"We had a hot misunderstanding over monetary issues." he pointed out. "Look! My deserted shop. I'm currently struggling! She took whatever she wanted to her parents without payment. I took a loan from the bank to try and rescue this sinking ship but she continued her misdeeds, milking me like I'm a dairy cow with very long protruding teats from a heavy udder." he stopped and snuffled. "I told her! She bankrupted me! I didn't have the amount she demanded, so she dumped these babies spitefully in return."

"It seems the babies are very hungry and they're tired of crying."

"She left them in the morning up to now. They're now suffering because of an unrepentant mother." he was emotional now.

Surely when two somnolent beasts in form of parents lock horns, it's the grass that suffers the most. I also observed a lot of men who have 'side chicks' who exist as second or third or fourth wives to their first wives. Nevertheless, the civil law in this country prohibits polygamy. Within this civilised era, it's now shameful to be a polygamist. Extra marital affairs culminate in disintegrated relationships.

I felt pity for Mr Chikopa but it was his own findings, but for the babies ... I felt like crying too because I was so touched. Their punishment was too much. From a swift calculation, the babies had endured almost six and half hours without breastfeeding. How I wish I was a philanthropist just like the First Lady who provides much needed support to Orphanage facilities. The mother of the twins portrayed a damnable character that proves she couldn't raise the children morally upright. How could she? She was a nuisance! Not capable of creating a conducive atmosphere for good upbringing of the twins. Mr Chikopa was snared by Jezebel into a great misery, actually he thought of the pleasure before his measure of the danger of indulging into extra marital relationships. The idea of chasing his first wife was very ignominious and uncalculated. It incubated a shot in his arm, the twinge in his guts, and a thorn in his flesh due to the mere fact that polygamy doesn't bring satisfaction and family tranquillity but it unleashes more complex problems.

A study conducted by the Institute for Family Studies revealed that docile women in such marriages have higher rates of HIV infection and sustain more domestic violence. Their life expectancy is shortened than that of monogamous ones.

People should follow the wise words 'One thread for the needle, one love for the heart' and desist from promiscuity.

Many of the vulnerable destitute kids in the streets came from such families. Some of them having been abandoned by their unscrupulous mothers who doesn't bear any care, and lack the essential mother's instinct. Baby dumping is a very serious case.

Sandra's abandonment of the one week olds at their father's workplace leaving him bereft hope is lesser evil though. Some new-borns are being forsaken in awful places shortly after coming into this world. Others are being derelicts in toilets, forests, bags etc. Considering our African society, the notion of deserting one's product is unfathomable.

But it happened at Tandai area near Cashel Valley. In the early hours of the day, a Marowa family went to harvest their maize field that was about a kilometre away from people's residence. They worked till sunrise and their dog smelled something, sniffed around and led Mr Marowa to discover a new born forlorn at the centre of the field. The scene was very bloody. He saw the placenta hanging precariously on a maize cob. The baby still had her umbilical cord attached. Flies had begun congregating on her head and on the umbilical cord. Her face was smeared with thick mud, upon removing mud from her mouth, she began crying alerting the other family members who then crowded the place. Mrs Marowa took the baby hurriedly to Mutambara Mission Hospital whilst her husband heading for Cashel Valley Police Station to report the case. At the hospital it was discovered that the baby was six hours old, she came on earth prematurely as well and in a critical health condition.

For most of us, the birth of a new baby is a celebrating happy occasion, but such was not the case when Theresa came on earth. By that time, my father a police sergeant teamed up with Assistant Inspector Katsuwa and embarked on *Operation where is your baby'* in that area. One older woman tipped them of a girl suspected to be pregnant but hiding it. They were also assisted by some villagers who knew all pregnant women in Tandai. The girl was then discovered with bloody clothes. There wasn't any need to consult a witchdoctor whether the girl was the one plain evil that gave birth and dumped a new-born in Marowa's maize field. She was arrested on the charge of attempted murder. After thorough interrogation, Theresa's mother unburdened that the baby was born out of the confines of marriage, so it was an attempt to prevent being shamed by the community. Miraculously, Theresa survived.

However some unscrupulous people misquote the biblical story of Moses. It's pathetic! They ruthlessly dump their babies in anticipation of Foundling Homes in their disorderly heads. It's by God's grace for the baby to be found alive and taken care of. A lot of abandoned babies are actually dying unattended! Moses mother's intention wasn't to kill him but she was compelled by Pharaoh's instruction on midwives and his army to kill all boys born by Israelite parents. She placed the Jewish infant in a reed basket and set him afloat. To show that she had care, she could come and breastfeed him regularly and instructed Miriam who happened to be Moses's sibling to stay hiding nearby watching the basket. Fortunately he was discovered and nurtured in King Pharaoh's house.

Nowadays it's very disheartening. In urban areas, some children are being discarded as if they were scratched juice cards. This has led to the increase of rakish Street Children who lack in moral restraints. They steal from both motorists and pedestrians. An unsuspecting motorist lost his mobile phone whilst making a phone call in a daylight robbery by Street kids at a robot intersection in Harare CBD. If you walk relaxing, you might fall a victim to those marauding glue dissipated thugs. Earlier in the day Christwish had told me, she also fell a victim in Harare CBD. Her boyfriend bought her a medium pizza. They hugged, but the medium sized pizza box was snatched in the process, only to later realise a small gourmand creature in ragged and oily clothes already enjoying the pizza licking his charcoal black fingers. What nauseated Christwish was the boy's wild behaviour. She said he sniffed glue whilst chewing the pizza, and later blurted out vulgar words. The pungent smells from the boy debilitated her.

The sprawling of wild street kids has jeopardised both motorists and drowsy pedestrians in most Cities across the globe.

"Go and report the case to the Police. These babies are too young and they don't deserve such treatment. Police officers will investigate and intercept her from wherever she is hiding." I said with great concern.

"I'm going to report the case. But she refuted the idea of abortion, but look! What she's doing now?" He blurted out a rhetorical in an emotional voice.

"Mr Chikopa! Abortion is a grave sin tantamount to murder!" Screamed Mrs Madziva.

The twins were not even safer under his custody. My skin crawled. It was very pathetic and frightening too. When they started crying furiously, I shivered as if I had got cold. And suddenly I found there were some tears squeezing out of my eyes.

CHAPTER 5

Part One

"Good morning Mr Manyika?" Audrey the Head girl greeted me as I stepped out from form One B' classroom.

"Good Morning Audrey?" I answered wondering what could have brought her to my class.

"Sir! I saw John Cearner coming out from girls' toilet!"

"What!"

"John Cearner and other two boys including Weber unscrupulously got into our toilet, I saw them coming out of the toilet. Someone said they were smoking weed."

"This is a very serious case, go and report directly to the Headmaster or Deputy."

"They're not available nor Mr Zabhura. They went to see Lucia who has been admitted at the Clinic." she said. Mr Mupanda the form Four A' class teacher was back at work, that's why I didn't know about Lucia's absence. Although I hated her for stigmatising the *'pregnant'* Mavis, my premonitions warned me there was something bad about her ready to explode.

"Where is he?" I asked rolling up my sleeves and clinching my fists.

"He ran into the orchard, usually he doesn't come back after smoking ... But he shouted out something." she revealed. "He said tell Mr Manyika to get ready for the fight. Any time is tea time!"

"What?"

"He said he want to revenge." said Audrey.

I bursted into an unprovocative laughter. "I think it's the effects of marijuana affecting his head."

Another girl came close by and said "Sir! They wrote on the inner walls of our Blair toilet. There're also some faeces on the outer edge of the wall. They wiped their backs using the edge of the wall instead of tissue paper or even tree leaves suggestively. They're deviances! It's not normal. I don't know why they are not getting expelled."

"They wiped using what?" I was scandalised.

"The edge of the toilet walls, proportionally to their heights. It seems they took turns." said the girl.

"It's abnormal. Okay don't worry girls. I will deal with them accordingly. Go back to your respective classes; we'll handle the case together with Mr Mupanda." A ghost of smiles seemed to cross their faces.

Another small boy came hurriedly "Sir! John Cearner and his company have fallen down from the big lemon tree in the orchard. They were scrumping lemons. They all fell hard from the top and started laughing uncontrollably but still they stumbled away. I'm quite sure they're seriously injured." said the little boy.

Why did they entered girls Blair toilet? Surely marijuana drives its user completely insane and the person loses all sense of moral responsibility. After excretion, how can a normal person wipe using the outer corner-edge of the toilet? John Cearner and his friends are under its influence. Why did they fell hard from the lemon tree and severely injured without any realisation of their condition? Weed bears very bad repercussions, it dispossess one's natural and normal will power leaving mentality ramshackle simulacrum to that of idiots. It usually culminate in untimely death. They were very lucky to escape death by a whisk after falling from tree top.

It all goes back to the slumbering community. Why allowing School children access illicit drugs? Why not whistle blowing, alerting the law enforcement agents? Drugs are being sold as if they were hot cakes whether in rural or urban setups. This has plunged the brighter future of students at stake. The faces of the future in form of children and young adults are being lost in the ugliness of the morally corrupt world! Why? Because drugs makes nonsense sense! It becomes a mammoth task for Educators to edify such drug addicts due to their high level of indiscipline. They're hard to teach.

Discipline increases an awaken student's abilities, skills and usefulness. As long as, we the citizens of this country don't collectively awaken and denounce drug usage, we'll be shooting ourselves in the foot, because drug abuse work hand-in-glove with other associated crimes. If we collectively shun substance abuse we can achieve sanity in our different communities. It seems a child who grows up in a poor neighbourhood with high rates of teenage delinquency and drug use is more prone to become a criminal than the ones exposed to a well compulsive moral society with a coordinated School system which distils them.

Drug abuse associated crimes are a very serious scourge that requires our active complement with law enforcement agents in a bid to wipe it off across all social strata, hence create an environment conducive to socio-economic development. Otherwise if societies remain sleepwalking, the future is doom and gloom.

"What were you doing at the orchard?" I asked the little boy.

"I was on punishment ... Collecting manure for the School garden."

"Okay go back to your class. I'll brief the Head. What's your name?"

"Silence Kondo, form One C." he paused and added. "One of them forgot this small plastic containing the Lilongwe product under the tree." he said whilst handing me a small plastic, those usually provided in clinics and hospitals containing tablets.

For a moment I scrutinized the greenish contents ... Ah Aah Aah! It was a high grade Malawian marijuana!

Part two

"I've called on Mr Zabhura to report the case to the Police "

"That's great! *John Tsvina* should be apprehended as soon as possible. We've to follow up on the case, because if we just stood on the side-line with our arms folded, the School might be turned into *a 'mogo fire'*" I said.

"That's the solution to completely circumvent this problem bedevilling Oxford Secondary" said Mr Mupanda.

"He's leading a very bad example, especially by his truancy"

"Some form Ones have also joined the truancy bandwagon. I've punished Silence Kondo a form One C' pupil for always being chronically late"

"Do you know, some families are culpable for their children's truancy"

"Children from lower income families with slumbering elders are more vulnerable to truancy because their parents tend not to be involved in their children's school life. They just recline and sleep" he said.

"Some of them can go extra miles by tasking their child too much laborious work before coming to School. For instance, they plough the field first and then come to school. They lose concentration at school."

"Yes it happens. The child can come to School late without bathing, reeking sweat. I don't know how they expect a child to succeed in educational attainment in such circumstances. You see! It's difficult to succeed if one misses too much School work and it culminate in pupil losing interest in School hitherto end in pitiful poor academic performance" he explained.

"But for John Cearner ... His truancy is being inflicted by substance abuse"

Mr Mupanda looked thoughtful and after a moment said "truant teens usually delve into serious criminal activities. I was deployed to Bumba Secondary School after graduation. We had so many students playing truant. Some of them started an association with dangerous gangs and later were involved in shoplifting. Those who were caught stealing were arrested and henceforth expelled from School. Others became dropouts and the ones left performed very poor academically. But I also blame the negligence of the community, because children easily accessed drugs ... At College there was also this young girl Violet. She was a napping truant. On a fateful day she vanished from College before lunchtime yet there were still crucial afternoon lectures. Very unfortunately she was kidnapped along a shortcut dusty pathway between maize fields on her way to see her sugar daddy alone from Mutare Teachers College. It happened within maize fields after Golden Peacock Hotel. Her head was found by a farmer in Natview Park near Sakubva River, but her body was never recovered. That served as a warning to other doping truants at College. People should be conscious in whatever they're doing regardless of their educational levels" said Mr Mupanda.

"All High School truants need a thorough beating. That's the only language they understand"

Part Two

Students were dismissed at one o'clock in the afternoon. They were very excited to be extricated earlier. Most of them were milling out of the School buildings, rushing home.

I was seated comfortably bearing Mr Zabhura and Miss Paradzai Company in the staffroom. Some of the teachers busied themselves preparing to travel for the weekend. Mrs Mombeshora and Mrs Nyagomo heading for Chikanga in Mutare. Mr Chimeri for Twenty Two Miles, Zimunya and Mr Vhurande for Ndima near Rusitu Mission. Mrs Mawuru has been complaining because of the skyrocketing bus fares but intended to travel all the way to Headlands. Mr Chesa has been also still pondering; it looks like he was in the same pot with Mrs Mawuru and intended to direct his foot to his rural home at Mabiya. Mr Mupanda had already traced his way back to Wengezi where his sick relative resided. Mr Chizemo was departing to Chayamiti. He was an anonymous-looking man, the sort who fades from your memory as soon as you've left him. But I don't think the same applies to his teachings, although he just looked bored and fed-up with his job. Christwish and Mrs Madziva were shilly-shallying.

The trio of us were busy marking students' written work. There was silence in the staffroom, broken only by the rustle of turning pages. The School was now deserted, tranquillity smoothly prevailing.

After twenty five minutes, Shylet broke the silence; "Mr Zabs you didn't briefed us about Lucia's condition?"

"What Mr Ruchiyo has done is utterly unacceptable! These businessmen! They wake and realise where their dangerous games will lead them." He said rhetorically after forcing a nonchalant little shrug.

There was a whole minute of dead silence. "What befallen Lucia?" I asked out of curiosity.

"Ruchiyo clambered up the ladder using improper means!"

"Please Mr Zabs, just go straight to the point." pleaded Shylet.

He hesitated as if debating how much he should tell us, then; "let me tell you the whole story." he said and cleared his throat. We both stopped marking, paying attention to Mr Zabhura's narration. "At first he offered his eye to the gods!"

"What!" I was shocked.

"He went on a rigorous rich making ceremony in Mozambique and offered his eye in the process. That's why he's deviantly left eyed. After the rituals, he came back home and ventured into the milling business. He bought a grinding mill. For some years he succeeded in the business and bought another one. When he went to the purveyor of charms to procure the magical means to lure lots of customers he was presented with a number of oaths. The first one was that he should not taste or eat meat for his whole life, any kind of meat even a grasshopper was prohibited. The second, he shouldn't bath. Third, he would be made infertile and forth he shouldn't use a constructed toilet, be it Blair, bucket, water system, pit latrine or any other form of toilet you might think of except bush. He chose the latter and came back home. People were very suspicious because he could drive his car at any time towards Guhune Mountains; I think that's where he used to relieve himself. When he was questioned about it, he argued, it was every person's right to go at a place wherever there's peace to make contact or supplicate God through prayers. But with much regret, he had already done enough to arouse people's suspicions. Nevertheless, others went on defending him saying the man was keeping the hotline with God, that's why he was speedy on becoming rich. In no time he bought a residential stand at Murambi low density suburb in Mutare and built a mansion. He never stopped the milling business here in Mandima until the Chiadzwa diamond days."

"He stole diamonds!" Blurted Shylet.

"No, there was an ignorant young man in possession of the precious stones who came at one of his grinding mills. The young man had three buckets of maize but without money to pay for the service. So he absentmindedly offered Mr Ruchiyo one piece of the worthy diamonds. After a few hours, those who nourished enmity towards him reported the case to the Police who then apprehended him for illegal gem possession. Whilst in police custody, there wasn't any way to relieve himself at the bush. I think he tried by all means to tie his bladder and intestines up to near bursting point and later gave up. He used the toilet inside prisoner's cell. That's when the hell broke loose. All the charms were spoiled and put to shame. A mysterious fire gutted his mansion in unclear circumstances at Murambi and his two grinding mills developed complicated mechanical faults. His successes collapsed. Somehow he was sentenced only four months in jail. After enduring his sentence, he came back home crestfallen. All his accumulated wealth has been plundered left to nothing. His wife vanished upon his arrival and he had to cope with five children on his own, including Lucia. The heaven only knew how he managed to coax someone to buy his faulty grinding mills, and managed to buy another one. However there was now a glimmer of hope that he would lead a faithful life but somehow he traced his foot back to Moza. He vowed to sacrifice his wife for the success of the business!"

"What!" Shylet exclaimed. She shivered and looking greatly perturbed said, "but why? And what has that got to do with the nourishment of the business? He was napping!"

"Miss Paradzai, you don't know the dirty works of some sloth business people." said Mr Zabhura.

"Well, I really don't know." replied Shylet with a shrug of the shoulders.

Mr Zabhura continued, "in no time Mrs Ruchiyo well known as Tabitha was killed by unknown people. She was found dead but seated under a tree by the roadside. Her nose and other body parts were missing. After some time the hell broke loose again, that's when the grinding mill started tripping and Mrs Ruchiyo's voice heard complaining, "I'm tired!" This happened continuously whenever the grinding mill overworked. But what surprised me were the villagers who continued to prefer Ruchiyo's grinding mill despite all the bizarre things which were happening. He married another young wife and opened a grocery shop but had a stiff competition from Chikopa. He had a number of affairs with women but he outclassed Ruchiyo. Green with envy and avarice, Ruchiyo again visited the purveyor of business charms, but this time around he wasn't offered a plethora of oaths to choose from. Instead, he was instructed strictly not to sleep during the night although there wasn't any effect if he sleeps in the morning or afternoon. He willingly vowed desisting from night sleeping, relocating his yearn for sleep to day. If he could by whatsoever means break that oath, he would face the music at its full blast. That package also included a live black goat's head with its eyes wide open, a decorated ritual brown clay pot and other witchcraft paraphernalia. It is said the head currently stay in the clay pot and supposed to be fed with milk only."

"How?" I asked

"They pour the milk into the clay pot and the goat's eyes would close if it's satisfied. If not satisfied, the eyes will remain wide open craving for more milk. The success of the business depends on the goat's head satisfaction."

"It's scary Mr Zabs! ... What are the consequences of breaking that oath?" Enquired Shylet.

"One of his children can die instantly or his current wife can run amok." replied Mr Zabhura.

"Mrs Ruchiyo must make sure that her husband doesn't sleep during the night by singing some songs for him to stay awake. So tell us, what happened to Lucia? ... They broke the rules of the charms!" Cried Shylet.

"Currently there's an adverse milk shortage in this country. It's said the goat's head had spent almost three days without drinking milk. The lethal part is that it would demand blood at the end." he said and totted. "Lucia is currently the victim. She was attacked by a severe stroke! But she's lucky to be alive. His relatives have openly castigated his daring misdeeds citing he's playing a very perilous game. If he wants to be rich he should work very hard and refrain from using lethal magical means."

"Have you tried to approach him?" I asked.

"After being castigated, his shoulders were stiff with suppressed rage. In his present red rage, nobody dared approach him."

"What about his young wife, Lucia's stepmother?"

"Nowhere to be found. She's now a mental patient. Yesterday Mr Ruchiyo slept during the night against his oath. It is said he spent the day enjoying whisky and at night he succumbed to sleep. Especially when someone is drunk, sleep when it comes cannot move on tip toes but on swift wings like some pestilence ridding the wind such that you had no time to think but only to give in to divorce from consciousness. His wife attended to Lucia, so she wasn't available to sing for him hence the consequence."

"It's just like living in jail under those oaths. Why can't he just return the charms or to burn the clay pot in Jesus name? Surely the love of money is the root of all evil." I said.

"He can't burn it if he wants to live. A close source has said the goat's head is talking, unleashing some death threats to his family." said Mr Zabhura.

Shylet felt a sudden stab of fear. "The goat's head talking!" She exclaimed. Her eyes had a way of retreating into her skull when she was very weary.

"What is it saying?" I asked curiously.

"For Lucia's recuperation, it is demanding ..." He stopped. There was a discreet knock on the staffroom door.

"Come inside!" Answered Shylet.

The person entered. She was Mr Zabhura's wife, smiling broadly towards her husband. "My Queen!" Mr Zabhura stood up from his chair. He touched her cheek, tilted her chin, smiled down at her and said "darling don't let the maid cook for me today. I'm craving for the taste of your food"

"Okay daddy, what do you prefer for a meal today?" Asked Mrs Zabhura. She smiled across at her husband, her mouth tremulous with love.

"You know my regular preference but today I want something different." he paused, thought for a minute in silence, "a very small sadza and goulash."

"Okay, can you accompany me to the shop to buy meat and some vegetables if you're not busy." she said and her husband nodded in agreement.

Part Three

Mr Ruchiyo's dangerous enterprises got on my nerves. I thought ... Is it a sign of the imminent eschatology? A lot of people desire riches but in return suffer from money 'sickness syndrome', often stressed with monetary issues. People have fallen victim to the ill effects of money-related anxieties especially in third world nations. If one slumber on wealth matters, it is highly probable that he or she become plagued by monetary worries in form of headaches, lack of appetite, unjustified anger, negative thinking etc. In a certain report titled 'The Meaning of Money' the researchers observed that some of us are 'highly motivated by money and controlled by Money'. This may lead to stress and neuroticism. I remember the days I worked at Mega Family, the Director of the Company was always stressed, even when the business was in smooth operation, you could only tell from his simple smile although we worked with spirit to please him. I then deduced that money doesn't have any connection with happiness but exacerbates one's vulnerability to the ill effects of it. We must desist from dazzling as money slaves for the betterment of health and peace of mind. On the other side of the coin, moderate wealth increases human happiness when it forks one out of abject poverty and into the middle class. However, those who always pin their hopes on accumulating wealth are prone to seek perilous and lethal magical means like what Ruchiyo did. A person should be satisfied with what he or she earns if enough to sustain his family and also avoid unnecessary debts.

I casted my eyes to Shylet and admired her dexterity on marking students' written work. She was very faster and methodic.

"Thomodia, what do those who seek magical means in whatever be it business or sports want to achieve?" Finally she broke the silence rhetorically enquiring.

"It's all about rich excessive desires."

"But why slumbering on consequences?"

"They're dazzled and lured by materialistic things and turn on a blind eye to the possible repercussions. Their mind's eyes are only focused on beautiful houses, posh fuel guzzling cars, latest fashion, delicious food varieties, flourishing businesses, latest computers and smartphones, beautiful ... really gorgeous women." I stopped because my tongue was really getting ahead of me.

"That's it!"

"That desire of possessing things is very perilous. It's happening! You know, someone can admire your dress and with no time she can come to borrow it for a wedding occasion, but her own wardrobe will be full of nice clothes."

"Brenda borrowed a dress from my sister for a special business meeting. She didn't return it for almost a month. My sister just kept quiet, but we got the wind that Brenda was always proprietorially using that dress when going to work. One day we went to an organised special party. We went there donning other clothes intending to change at the venue. My mother was also invited, so she was there. We were given a room to change our clothes and put on the special ones. Brenda opened her bag, laid out that beautiful dress, then her knickers, her bits of jewellery, hurryingly out of her former clothes, she took her makeup and walked over to the mirror over the dressing table. We were almost eight women in that changing room. When she was busy applying her makeup, my mother touched the dress and scrutinized it pensively. Leaving the mirror, Brenda came back to the bed, slid the dress over her shoulders, sucking in her mouth to keep her lipstick smooth, that's when my mom bursted out, hurled at her some insults and took off the dress from her after a skirmish."

Surely some people imply false impressions. Nowadays it's ignominious to publicly use borrowed or even donated clothes. Those who go to some churches really understand it. Someone might pompously raise you up to show all congregants the nice shoes or suit he gave you because you're poor. You have to be humble enough and not to indulge into proposing girls because anytime you'll be picked up and raised to show other congregants a shirt you accepted from the church's charity organising committee. Dazzling around with such things is now synonymous with nakedness because he'll be pointing at you from a distance showing all and sundry the good she did to you. It's high time to work hard for the crucial things we crave for, and look all our demons straight in the eye. But our cravings shouldn't go against our principles.

"It's pathetic! So what happened after your mother took the dress?" I asked.

"Brenda didn't attend the party, she went back home melting in embarrassment ..." She paused and abruptly enquired after some few seconds in silence, "What are you going to eat for supper?"

"I don't know, I might poach Zabhura's goulash."

I didn't like what his wife is doing, you heard Zabhura complaining. Their maid is the one who does everything. He might be snatched by the maid if his wife continues sleeping, surrendering crucial roles on the maid's shoulders. A married woman must cook and wash for her husband despite the presence of a housemaid. Couples often tangle on such issues. My aunt's marriage was jeopardised by an all-weather friendly maid. She could outclass her and that led my uncle adore her to an extent of considering to make her his mistress. Their marriage was in shambles, really shambolic! But my aunt was put to shame because all she knew was tattling with other women in their neighbourhood. In return, her marriage was left in tatters. Charlene's mother is slumbering like what my aunt did. One day Zabhura will not complain openly but he'll just fall for the maid because ..."

I interjected her, "because maids possess the values and qualities expected from a woman. But I don't think Mr Zabhura can do that. He is a well esteemed man."

"I've noticed you developed a rapport with him, but I know men. He can do it! He could be just fed up with always complaining. Don't you know that house helpers are breaking drowsy women's marriages?"

I thought for a moment and finally realised it also happened to my own aunt's marriage. "So you mean Zabs would tend to seek comfort from the housemaid?" I asked, whilst my mind was busy opening up some files to get the details of how her marriage was left ramshackle by a maid, but not exonerating her philander husband.

"Men are lustful, so there's no concrete reason to justify or ignore such a thing. My main concern is on Mrs Zabhura's weakness of letting the maid take complete control of the kitchen."

"Yes, you're right Shylet. Married women must cook for their husbands. The best way to a man's heart is through his stomach, the house maid will cook for him and in the process win his affection."

"When I get married I won't hire any form of a maid. I would rather juggle all the chores by myself. If it becomes too much its better use his relative."

"Because you're jealous Shylet!" I fetched up a laugh and added, "you already doubt your fiancé even before getting married. Trust is the sole foundation as well as the pillar of a lasting relationship."

"I'm awake Thomo! Prevention is better than cure. I just want to avoid problems that might arise."

As if I had been searching and feeding scraps of information to some hidden computer in my mind and now suddenly the memory of my aunt's marriage popped up. For her, the issue of house helpers revoke some nasty memories. Trinity the maid was hardworking and had the ability to juggle all the chores. My aunt's family was not cohesively bonded. Why? As the lady of the house she could've trained herself and be in a better position to effectively take on chores like cooking and washing, as it is a great way to bond with family and explore the motherhood. Chidembo her husband was snatched by the maid but she blames herself for being too sluggard and naive in considering her husband faithful. She was married for almost eight years and never had any issues with her husband, but after nursing her third born she decided to go for College to further her education but against her husband's will. Later Chidembo gave her the green light and suggested a nearby Mutare Polytechnic, but she was very adamant on her preference Harare Polytechnic. She got a maid to do the house chores and other domestic works prior her departure to Harare.

Some months later, Chidembo grew close to the maid and it culminated into a love affair. It took her a very long time to notice since she was always away at Harare Poly unaware and unsuspecting things which were happening in her matrimonial home. But eventually one day all hell broke loose when she was supposed to travel back to Harare from Mutare after the vacation. There was a downpour on that day, the rain was really furious. She forgot her credentials only to realise halfway at Headlands. She decided to travel back home and that's where she got the scandalisation of her life.

The rainfall still poured furiously from the clouds and almost midnight when she got home at Gimboki. She entered the living room and found the baby forlornly crying and that was enough to arouse her suspicions. She opened her bedroom, but didn't find Chidembo. She embarked on a search for him all over the house but couldn't find him, and then decided to wake Trinity to enquire why she desolated the baby, and on opening the room she found both Chidembo and Trinity without any piece of thread on their bodies and passionately kissing snugly lying together. Immediately she divorced him. She couldn't have the guts to forgive him, because to fall in love and sleep with their house helper in their matrimonial home was beyond excruciating and humiliating.

My own aunt slumbered, and her husband too. Sleeping with the house maid is extremely disrespectful to the wife, especially doing it from the matrimonial home. Above it all, it's a big sin caused by the weakness of one's heart. We've to guard against Somnambulism on such issues, even biblically; those who are standing are exhorted to be careful not to fall. Marriage is supposed to be sacred. Of course! Evil spirits always work for excess hours to derail one's determinations. So one needs to be always awake and conscious. The man and his wife should be both faithful to each other because even the Bible admonish that the marital bed is supposed to be kept holy and no one should defile that.

If a man somnolently falls for the maid, she can start behaving as a co-wife and even go extra miles of hatching plans to do harm to the wife and her children.

But overally, I deduced that some married women are the root causes of the problem as they exploit their lacking's and incapability's in handling even the tiniest of house responsibilities. When she show that she's not capable of handling the home, and her husband will start viewing her as a less of a woman then pick a special interest in the other one who can handle house responsibilities.

Also some women have a weakness of great somnolence by letting maids take complete control of their families, especially in the kitchen. Some somnolent unscrupulous sloth house ladies let their maids clean their bedrooms, wash the husband's underwear and even make the bed, initiating temptation for their own husbands.

I wondered on how Shylet could carry out all the house chores with her ambition to become White. I know of some young ladies like her, who just crave to look more beautiful and sit in living rooms like decorations whilst barking instructions to maids capable of juggling all the house chores. For instance some of them hire about three or four maids, one for cooking, one for washing, one for cleaning and sweeping, one for playing with the kid plus a gardener. It all depends on money, but actually how can a man respect such a sloth? One who doesn't cook! All she can do is to command and sleep. Umm! It all depends on choices, so let me not delve into it too much of it. Choices differ. But how do they? They even make the maids clean their bedrooms! A place which is supposed to be private. What they know best is how to go shopping and gossiping with neighbours. Its high time women should wake up and smell the coffee, taking charge of their homes by carrying out their responsibilities.

I casted back my eyes on Shylet who had gone back on her marking dexterity. "There're also some men possessed by an adulterous evil spirit who can go for the neighbour's maid." I said to myself.

CHAPTER 6

Part One

Two or three hours now, the people had waited. They had waited patiently for the arrival of WFP (World Food Programme) donated food items. The time was two and half hours before midday. The weather was comfortably hot. A lot of people were milling into the School yard, others were already at the School football ground where the goods were going to be received.

Some were engaged in group discussion under some trees. Under a tree nearby the Administration Block were four men discussing about the death of Mr Ruchiyo's youngest child, who had just passed away in the earliest hours of the day. I remained rooted at the Admin entrance to hear more details of bizarre things transpiring within Ruchiyo family. One of them mealy-mouthed on the real details of the latest death. But the arrival of a fifth man saw the details being unearthed.

"Yesterday Lucia was transferred to Mutambara Mission Hospital." The man said. "She was accompanied by her father to Mutambara since you already know that her step mother ran amok. Upon arrival at the hospital, Lucy was immediately admitted. It was almost dusk. The whole drama happened at midnight when Ruchiyo sneaked into the female ward to check on his daughter. The nurses saw him up and down the ward, moving restlessly to avoid sleeping but sister Mujati the nurse on duty mistaken him for a mental patient and pierced him with some sleeping injections and totted some sleep tablets. She wasn't aware that Ruchiyo vowed not to sleep during the night. Within some few minutes, he fell down and eventually succumbed to sleep. He was then carried to a male ward where he slept comfortably. I think his business charms were soiled and put to shame because it's his second time to sleep at night within the same week. This has ensued to the death of his youngest child, but it is said Lucy is still agonising alive. The problem is the starving goat's head."

The other man interjected, "that evil goat is responsible for the child's death. It's now relying on blood."

Their conversation was cut short as they noticed a convoy of Lorries that were bouncing and rattling up the hill towards the School. In a trice the men rushed to the football ground.

As the first lorry approached, people gathered and started whistling and ululating. Excited voices were raised. The four vehicles slowed and stopped in the middle of the ground. The drivers climbed out, shook hands with Village Heads, broadly smiling. There was a concerted movement towards the back of the Lorries, loaded with much needed food stuffs. Cords were untied and tents were ripped off. One by one; mealie meal, cooking oil boxes, tinned fish packs, matemba, beans and some cow peas were passed from hand to hand into the pitched tent.

I received a phone call from Mrs Madziwa informing me that Barbra her young sister had arrived and immediately wanted to meet me in quest for English remedial lessons. I told her to meet me at my classroom, form One B' since I was in possession of the keys.

She was a large girl, generously fleshed with attractively enormous lips. Her eyes were very beautiful, with long lashes that were her own. She got into the classroom alone. Dressed in a tight shirt and a bikini Jean. Her flesh flowed smoothly, curves and limbs artfully crafted. She looked around the classroom and sighed, and forced a smile that lightened up her beautiful face. Already an intense happiness filled my heart making me ecstatic, almost exultant. Looking at her, she looked like a girl gripped by *love at first sight* magnet. I also took the bait. She smiled again, and this alone was enough to make me feel exuberant. There was a certain magnetism about her that filled me with a desire to possess her. But at the same time, my mind's eye could picture a bad and frivolous English student. I glanced around the classroom and she also followed suit. Her enormous eyes were wild and excited. My blood chanted wild dissonant tunes that covered my ears like a foreign song especially when she began moving slowly towards the Teacher's desk where I was uncomfortably seated. Her's was no ordinary beauty. She drew closer. The closeness and the mellifluous voice did things to me and I found myself squirming on the chair.

We conversed and I discovered in due course that she had a mind as sharp as a whetted blade. Her English Language failure was due to sickness on the examination day, but she scooped the highest grades in all other ten subjects including Maths.

She was a jolly soul and pleasant company.

I decided to start by giving her an essay, *'The day when all hell broke loose'*. She took the front desk; usually the one occupied by Chiedza, lowered her bulk, filled the whole chair, and started writing. She struggled to amply handle a pen; her nails were so long they didn't seem to end. They were artificial. Her handwriting was good though I thought it was going to be chicken scratch. As of late I thought of all beautiful girls as dumbest birds, nothing more than air-heads and bimbos, had their big breasts largely un pro rata to their brains. Size sixty tits, size two brains.

But for Barbra a genius, it seemed her brains were just as big as her breasts. Happy to live a celibacy life, I had found no excuse to propose to a girl and so now I didn't know how to proceed. The only logical way to circumvent this problem, I realised, was to do nothing, let things take the natural course, just drift with the tide. And, that's what I did meekly. Her long dark black hair fell down over her forehead as she shook her head, and she raised a hand to push it back. You know! There're some gestures that women do that make them amongst the most graceful of animals.

She completed writing the essay. Her handwriting was painstaking and her spelling perfect. She wrote a very scintillating story of how she had been in an intimate love relationship with her English Teacher named Manyika, but one day their love affair was discovered by her sister through some love text messages found in her cellphone. Barbra used my name in her essay! I stared at her with uncomprehending eyes. Almost as if she had read my thoughts, she blurted "I used your name for a purpose Mr Manyika!" She smiled angelically, biting the ends of her fingers.

I felt confused and off balance like a ship caught in a tempestuous storm. Her actions caused me a complex problem and so unexpected it threw me out of my stride. She could afford to indulge all her wildest fancies. I could not, I thought. I was not even dreaming but experiencing cold reality. A pulsating anger began to grow, tying up my gut into a cold knot but her smiles somehow soothed me like a tranquilliser. Taking stock of my situation, I realised there was nothing I could do. We continued with the lesson.

It was a *One on One* lesson. Yes! *One on One* with the man of God! We were the only two in the classroom. From the essay to grammar and some vocabularies we finished the lesson.

She enquired on the charges of my services but I refuted to charge her any money. She thanked, really appreciating and to my biggest scandalisation she came very close to me and planted her enormous lips against mine and I froze. It grew and I jerked my head away violently. She then looked at me in a way that put the fear of God into me. My heart started pounding like a hammer as if it would jump out of my chest, my breath coming fast and hot, making my mouth dry as the desert sands.

She walked towards the closed door deliberately slowly, swinging her hips. Standing at the door with her arms akimbo, she displayed her strong white teeth that later went with a laugh she fetched up from her guts. "Do you fear women?" She asked and kept looking at me.

I clenched my hands and replied, "my dear! Women are not exactly a closed book to me."

In return she smiled broadly. Abruptly she closed her eyes, "ooh my eye!" She cried.

"What happened to your eye?" I asked anxiously.

"Please come and help me remove this eye lash out of my eye. Please!" She cried, whilst trying to shove it with her handkerchief.

I went to her, she bent her head. Actually taking an eyelash out is a close-up project. My eyes stared directly into her eyes at close range. I promptly spotted the eyelash and edged it towards the corner. Just about in time I got it out and shifted away, short of breath.

Frankly I told her not to come for the lessons ever again. I loathed her dragon tattoo on her neck. She opened the door, waved a goodbye, smiling ruefully and tore down the path to her sister's house. Later I also tore down the pathway that led to the football ground to try and get the thing out of my system.

After this incident I was very depressed. I was initially tempted and took the bait and awakened prior swallowing it. Barbra wasn't a good girl. I also wondered why these days' parents and guardians stand aside and watch while the values of this generation's girls are going to the dogs.

I knew my blockage of the future English lessons disgusted the devil, Satan, for its mission to lead a lot of people away from God. When people go wrong, he celebrates and ululates in uncontrollable joy. He loves to see children lose focus and decency, honour, respect and responsibility. I'm much aware that when he works, he uses various machinations. If I had noticed that Barbra was the devil's agent, I shouldn't have been wooed at the first place because of the devil's ambassador's badge on her neck. I accidentally fell for her and realised immediately that she was a tart. The whole issue started nauseating me. I don't know why some School girls have gradually developed no sense of decency and moral hygiene.

I also shared the same sentiments with the one Morris Mtisi who also highlighted in Manica Post that nowadays readers or entertainment lovers are stupidly excited about and in love with obscenity especially sex related content. This has damaged students' morals to corrupted minds simulacrum to that of their bad sister Barbra. God forbid! Most of our celebrities in the entertainment industry are promoting sex! Why? Sex sells like hot cakes! Illicit drugs too. This has plunged morals futile. Student's minds are jeopardised by such things. The biggest problem being the entertainment business embedded in selling sex and drug related things creating a gloomy atmosphere for the future of young people. Yes of course I know! This world seems will not creep back to old days of good boys and girls but there's high need for consciousness among the youths no to just drift with the immoral tide. People don't care nowadays in what they write or what they sing. It's about attracting readers, listeners and buyers to get lots of money ... Not to help cultivate manners within this corrupted world. I'm of the opinion that as youths we should stop resembling as if we possess the least brain cells in our skulls. It's high time to cease considering those who are publicly indecent as celebrities, but deduce that mental derangement isn't a trademark of a celebrity. I'm quite convinced that Barbra's actions were contributed by seeing indecent movies. It's very disheartening! A lot of students are asleep whilst following ambassadors of the devil by indecently dressing and indulging in illicit drug consumption along with student prostitutions.

As a whole, we need to awaken to change our mind-sets and walk in the right direction for the betterment of our lives. It's high time we look our demons straight in the eye and strive for a way, where there's sense and meaning and realise the essence of responsibility and discipline.

As I tore down the path I was absorbed in a thought and realisation of how *One on One* lessons are perilous especially with the people of opposite sex. The thoughts crowded my mind like ants on a moist lump of sugar. A lot of parents are drowsily sending their girl Childs to *'One on One's*. Yes! In that kind of a lesson a child can learn and understand better but her future might be jeopardised by a lustful male teacher. Lessons can be converted into love conversations and the office or classroom into a love nest. Other girls might grew fond of the Educator and get obsessed. Its high time parents should wake up.

But on my part, I never stopped wondering where exactly I had gone wrong. Of course, there were so many ways I could have wiggled my way out of the snare. Being lured by her beauty was more like being caught between the devil and the crocodile infested dam. A raw inexplicable guilt assailed me, but it wasn't my fault. If I did wrong by falling for her, assume that we all make mistakes, we had to learn as we went along. I had learnt a very good lesson and always in future. I would remember, all beauties are snares!

At first, I was found in betwixt a rock and a hard surface. Others might ponder it was a lifetime chance. But I scrupulously considered it a temptation. But mind, I don't aim to be stared at through a microscope like a bacteria simply because I've my own likes and dislikes. But still what the flaming hell does it matter? That I didn't ride the horse! Nobody can be hypnotized against his will, I have a morality of some sort about that game.

Barbra had some dragon tattoos on her neck; I couldn't turn a blind eye on those imperfections. The thought that I didn't know her brought me back to more reality with the jolt of a million sharp knives. And, still carrying out this forced post-mortem of the incident, I realised that all were part of a plot, one had been cleverly plotted by the devil.

Part Two

"She did the same to me!" Said Mr Zabhura.

We were seated under a tree, observing how the WFP employees were conducting their business. Also as teachers, we were the last to receive the goods. We were also there on behalf of other absent teaching staff members. Mr Zabhura looked around conspiratorially and said, in a voice that had dropped to a whisper, his face pensive, "you see! Barbra is a *'She devil'*"

"What!" I exclaimed.

"She is a snake! I also discovered she's HIV positive." he said. Suddenly, I began to feel violated, weary and wasted. But I hid my feelings as best as I could. He totted, "you can't get HIV because of her lips planted on you though"

I felt relief washing over me, but making me weak on my knees. I'm diffident about prying too much into another man's private life, but a great curiosity preyed on my mind itching to know what transpired between him and the *'She devil'*. After a while I looked at him. He seemed to be deep in thoughts as if meditating. There was a faraway look on his face.

My mind was just about to start spinning, so I closed my eyes for stability. *'She devil'*! The name itself struck me in the face like a living force. There was a whole minute of silence. Then he said, "she blew me an unforgettable kiss! She is a different character possessing various characteristics. What happened is, she requested a History *One on One*, some time back towards her final O' Level examinations. I agreed to her request but it was utterly a big mistake." A certain amount of Mr Zabhura's present peace of mind evaporated. He sucked his bottom lip as if considering how much he should tell me, "she possess a bunch of tactics to woo men. Her beauty, intelligence as well that mellifluous voice is her biggest weapon. She came to me with a good character. She was a shy girl. But our *One on One* was riskier than most ..." He paused and started scratching his chin. I shivered as if I had got cold. At that moment we heard a voice calling us. She was a WFP employee calling and beckoning at us. We hurriedly went to collect the goods in the pitched tent.

After the WFP had gone, I was approached by a drunkard. I was standing outside the tent on guard of the food stuffs, waiting for Mr Zabhura who had gone to look for a wheelbarrow.

With a wide grin and a handshake that almost crushed my fingers, he introduced himself as Ford. He has a face similar to that of the naughty John Cearner. Though he was a nondescript man of an indeterminable age, and looking at him, one got the unnerving feeling that he had tried to commit suicide and failed. Ford was almost intoxicated. It didn't took long for him to introduce his story. He was in need of village whisky but had no money, so he offered me all the food stuffs he had just received for an amount of money equivalent to a two litre village whisky. That was very cheap, but I refuted the offer. Why? Because he was in a daylight slumber. How could a normal person trade a kilogramme of kapenta, 10kg mealie meal, 2l *Raha* cooking oil and some cow peas on top of that, just for 2l village brew? He was a sleepwalking alcohol slave. Isn't it?

It's happening in most families! If the man is addicted to the wise waters, the family usually suffer. Family bond is adversely affected, I thought.

He persisted, "Just five dollars Mr Teacher, you can take all this stuff." he pleaded but I was unencumbered.

"Do you have a family?" I asked.

"Yes! A very big one ..." He paused and added. "two wives and five kids."

"So why don't you go with the things home and feed your family?"

"Look my man! There're incessant squabbles within my family. My stress is only cured by village whisky. If I go home drunk, I won't be troubled or bothered so much." he blubbered.

I loathed his unconsciousness in handling his polygamous family. He was a mere dunce. I thought the food stuffs were the best treatment for his family's disputes. Sometimes food, when put on the table can ease problems. I don't know why he prioritised beer like that, at the expense of two wives and five kids. Upon realising that I was adamant, he retired and hurled at me some piercing insults before he staggered away. I remained aplomb.

That's why the Bible condemned the immoderate use of alcohol. I was insulted for no apparent reason. God forbid!

All what transpired were all in the huge lizard eyes of a man who was just nearby. He was a short swarthy man and had a remarkable complete bald head that sat comfortably on his broad shoulders like a brown, almost maples globe.

He approached. "I'm sorry Mr Teacher, that drunkard is my nephew. I didn't intervene because he is usually tempest and have violent tendencies whenever he is drunk." he said apologetically.

I took a moment and replied, "no it's okay, I know these drunkards very well" I said, with my voice coming out discordantly, I could hardly recognise as my own. Actually it sounded unfamiliar as if I had borrowed it from a stranger. He looked scared, obviously having witnessed my struggle for mental and emotional balance. "You've to sit down and talk to him. He's leading a very bad life. But I wasn't offended by his insults." I was lying and I also knew that he knew that I was lying. I was really offended.

Realising I had somehow become privy; he smiled weakly, his small rat-eyes searching for mine. He felt accommodated and unburdened his story. "You see! Mr Teacher. I was once a well-known big drinker. They nicknamed me *Musiyadzasukwa*. Surely I could leave the place after beer drums and calabashes were washed. But later, I realised that I was sleepwalking. Almost all the money I earned was spent on alcohol. In my house we had no furniture, so we used to sleep on the floor. I started drinking beer at a very tender age. By form two, I was now drinking constantly, and I became aggressive although it gave me a feeling of independence. I could drink up to five litres of village whisky per day. When I married, my drinking caused some big problems in my marriage. I could beat her and the children" he stopped and wiped a sweat beaded bald and continued "But when I woke up and quit drugs, my family welfare improved with a great deal. I struggled for some months and succeed in overcoming my alcohol problem. By reinstating back to conscious and shunning my slavery to alcohol, I am now able to buy furniture"

"What had motivated you to start drinking at such an early stage?" I enquired.

"Our forefathers were great drinkers and alcohol addicts, so we grew in that gloomy atmosphere of prioritising wise waters up to undesirable extents. The degree of drunkenness was unedifying. Friends could return me home dead dangling in a wheelbarrow. The same with my nephew Ford. His life is in an inferno. It's pathetic!"

"I can see you're now a template to other excessive drinkers but don't you still itch for it?" I asked.

"The desire for village whisky still lingers within me. But it only requires intense prayer and determination in order to stay awake and vigilant" he pointed out "drinking again would mean digging my own grave".

Before I asked him some more questions, Mr Zabhura came back with the wheelbarrow. The questions I had formed died somewhere deep in my throat, unasked.

The weather was now not as favourable as it had been in the past hours of the day. The sun was scorching, really blazing. We packed the goods and hurriedly to the teachers compound.

Part Three

He looked at me almost pityingly for some seconds without saying anything, then his face broke into a rueful smile "I want to tell you something and make a prognosis"

"Go ahead Morgie." I said. Everyone used to call him Morgie the janitor.

"As men we've to be more conscious nowadays. You're very lucky you didn't swallow the bait ..." He paused and took a deep breath. "She also did the same to me!"

"What!" I exclaimed and said, "I didn't have that. You're saying what?"

"She's very dangerous! She did the same to me. But inside the toilet" he said. I started feeling nervous as a pregnant baboon caught in a forest fire. He continued, "I once found her, one of the patrons at Madziro bar. You know that Madziro is a convenient hunting ground for lovers for the female flesh. I was drinking steadily with a friend of mine, for about an hour when I saw her. She approved and accepted my friend's Love curriculum vitae instantly. That's when I got some suspicions but later averted my mind about it. One day we met here in Mandima lest did I know she is Mrs Madziva's young sister? She requested for assistance to kill a snake inside a Blair toilet. So I went there armed with my catapult and how exasperated I was when I discovered that it was a lizard. I killed it though. After that, she furtively entered into that toilet to observe me throwing the thing into the pit. She planted her enormous lips on my forehead to my shock. I don't want to delve into details but I just want to alert you. There're some snares like her out there!"

"What do you mean Morgie?"

"She possesses an unarguably beautiful face any woman would kill to have but she's risky."

"Where is that friend of yours, whose CV approved and accepted instantly?" I enquired

"Deep-sixed!" He exclaimed and added, "he's now food for maggots. He only had few minutes affair with her, but that's when he threw his life at stake. I don't know why some men crave for those ladies of the night who linger around bars. Is it because of beer which impairs judgement? My friend Makuwaza was lured by that young age but, how was he to know, then, that he had just committed a very grave mistake. Surely, after the deed is done, consultation is useless. He became a recipient of a life prolonging medication which he later abandoned. That girl! ... She is an anopheles mosquito recklessly infecting any sleepwalker ..." He paused whilst opening a king sized Fanta bottle. He was vividly thirsty. But I was getting his point though, crystal clear, Makuwaza didn't took the ARVs maybe out of shy or else.

He continued, "One needs to be on high alert when dealing with nowadays girls. Despite their ages, some of them are perceived as good children during the day, but at night they nocturnally display their true colours by parading themselves in varying degrees of nudity. I heard it's happening at higher learning institutions. I couldn't have stomached three or four years of University but I really know that, there, some girls linger unabashed in micro-mini skirts that reveal more than what they cover. What's your opinion Manyika? You see! That's where highest rates of new HIV infections are being recorded. Morally, can one fully enjoy the fruits of her education after being infected with AIDS by a sugar daddy? ... Some college girls are just somnolent due to excessive love of money but at the end she awaken after getting pregnant and infection ..."

I interjected him, "others might be finding men, who can fund them throughout the course hitherto succeed in degree attainment."

"Then it's like soliciting the devil to carry you on his back, on your way bound to heaven." he laughed a loud bark.

"I got it. It's more like some of our sisters tend to lose control over their moral faculties when they go to universities. More like having hallucinations on love issues. Yet morals corrode. This also applies to boys who then delve into drug abuse. How can a drug addict peacefully enjoy life? I don't know why our Pastors are failing to deal with these issues at Higher Learning Institutions." I inquired rhetorically.

"Aah! Those same pastors who burn with evangelical fire on the pulpit when they sermonize on morality, condemning student prostitutions and drug abuse, crawl out at night to hunt, surreptitiously, those female students who provide the exact sins at night" revealed Morgan.

"D'you mean we've spurious Pastors nowadays?"

"And fake churches as well!" He protested. "Fake churches are actually straying from the mission that Jesus Christ gave"

"What are they doing? It seems you don't have a church of your choice"

"Aah my young bro! Can't you see that these days Churches are more of joy providers, in form of entertainment and secular attractions rather than instructions from the Bible? There're a lot of sleepwalking churchgoers in this corrupted world. Lots of Preachers are after substantial income and the gospel of prosperity' is their popular theme which woos the dopey ones. What I mean is that, congregants are told that they will become very wealthy and healthy if they contribute generously to the church. So as a result, a lot of people pour in huge sums of money, for those scams, who in turn enrich themselves" he took a deep sigh and drank from his bottle "umm politics also! In a church! National politics are introduced, often clearly and specifically. Are they real churches?"

"You're right Morgie! Why do they also invite celebrities? Huh! A visiting celebrity! A morally corrupt minded one, on top of that. Other churches go an extra mile by inviting some dancehall artists to entertain their congregants with dirty lurid lyrics. I thought these churches are being formed in a bid to preserve the little that remains of our moral and Godly fabric, but in actual sense they're exacerbating the problem. They're just after making money. Sexual perverts too! The suits and church belts they put on every Sunday doesn't remind them of the need to be exemplary" I said.

"God is often presented as tolerant of whatever! But what irked me most are fake miracles. Some well-rehearsed dramas! After all, people are made to pour their hard earned cash after being weakened by the charms."

"Yes, some churches are using magical means to drain cash from somnolent congregants. I often hear some people testifying that once you get into the territory you get clinched by the offering or pledging spirit. Some go back to their dwellings on foot after offering all the money to the last cent." I said and looked back at him, but now wondering what had brought him to my house.

We had been seated inside my kitchenette for almost half an hour and so far Morgan had not got to the point of his visit. Since I came to Mandima, he had never visited me, so I wondered because he stayed a kilometre away from the School. We were not friends, but we were friendly. He seemed to be on easy terms with everyone around the School. As if he had heard what I had been thinking, as if I had been thinking aloud, he abruptly sighed. There was some strain around his eyes and a distrait look I hadn't noticed for the time we had been together.

He idly flipped through a magazine lying on his laps, the delaying action of a man who wants to exchange confidences but doesn't know how to start. I had observed that he had a gift of jest, but not when it came to requesting for help. He drank from his bottle, then looked down at the amber liquid in it, one eye closed as if it were a microscope. He was a tall fat man in his early thirties and he was remarkably handsome, but he seemed completely unaware of his looks. But he had a permanent black scar on his forehead though. Dressed in a blue work suit, he looked so healthy and invulnerable to illness, but now looked acutely miserable.

He took another drink, sat staring at the bottle again "Samanyika ... Would you buy this device." he raised his tablet.

"What would I do with another smartphone?"

"Listen Samaz, I'm not asking the earth. I just want enough to clear my debts."

"Right now I'm impecunious."

He took a deep breath and blurted. "I'm on hard times. My son, Wisdom was sent home from Thabanchu Primary, I haven't yet paid for his school fees. My landlady is also about to chase me, she is currently grumbling due to close to four months of unpaid rentals. I borrowed some food stuffs from Ruchiyo's shop. Chikopa is also wielding an axe. I ordered that tailor Mishy Chibhamu to make my wife and children's' matching outfits, she's done. Several women are also seething because of unpaid dues for their wares. Aah ah I also borrowed money from Mr Mutseiwa ... Aah and from Mr Khumbula too! ... Ugh sorry Manyika ... For wondering out loud. I was more talking to myself." He grinned a little. "I've come snivelling to you with my troubles. Actually I don't think I can kill my own snakes." he smiled ruefully in embarrassment.

What a long chain of debts! I had to ask him, "Aren't you listed on the payroll?"

"I'm being paid yes, from the School coffers ..." He hesitated. "I bought this tablet worth six hundred US dollars on credit. That's where all my salary is channelled to." He said remorsefully. His revelation nearly ejected me out of my chair. I stared hard at him and he was grinning inanely, almost idiotically, back at me. He then sighed wearily and blurted "oh, my God! I'm living a dog's life." He cried and groaned, and I thought he looked like a man who had swallowed a bee.

But why plunging into such ignominious debt? Isn't it a drowsy-walk? How I wish, those who are absurdly incautious against the trappings of obsessively pursuing materialistic things of this world, leading to such humongous debts be struck by a bolt of God's white light, the same it did in the biblical story of Paul.

A lot of people are plunging themselves into debts and possess a list as long as the original snake of unpaid debts whilst leading a fake lifestyle. Why admiring those who dexterously twiddle their fingers on pricey high-end smartphones yet having a family responsibility that should shut that mind? After all, why starving the family just for WhatsApp bundles with the desire of gossiping, no business at all? In urban circles, some aren't seeing the irony of buying fuel guzzling cars to drive to work when their landlord uses foot for their daily errands. Why not saving to buy own house? Some unscrupulous ones would rent a commodious apartment in upmarket leafy suburbs, where ordinarily they could have used the money to buy a house of their own. Isn't it misplaced priority? Why drifting with the tide and leading a fake lifestyle too? Whilst Parents languishing in poverty back home! Probably those guys need their heads examined!

I remember very well of a Gurenje couple. It was a model couple in Cashel Valley who could come to church in nice matching outfits, attracting everyone's attention. The duo was one of the biggest funders of church related activities. On one very unfortunate day, their eldest son of twelve years of age was involved in a serious bicycle accident and fractured his knee. I visited him at the hospital. I couldn't help, but eavesdrop on the agonising relatives-having been forced to make some contributions for surgery and to buy medicines - on why the couple didn't have a Medical Aid for the seriously injured kid. There were even more revelations that the couple had bought an exorbitantly priced iPhone for their church Bishop recently and left impecunious.

Whilst I was taking a stroll down the memory lane, Morgan's tablet rang, "haa hallo halloo Ma'am." he answered the call.

His phone was on hands free; I heard an aged woman's voice at the end of the wireless, "Hie Morgie! Your little sister brought a letter from the School saying they now want the money for fees or else they'll expel her from School. We're surviving on mealie rice, we don't have money to pay grinding mill. We've only one gallon maize left, no soap at all. We no longer knew the taste of cooking oil in vegetables. Please don't forget that money we borrowed from Mai Tasa its now three months overdue. Remember also my bus fare, I need to go and collect BP medications. I need to see a doctor too and ..."

The call had broken. He took a moment deep in reflected thought and looked up, his eyes shining as if he was pretty close to tears. Abruptly he stood up in despair, now tears quite plain in his eyes.

Part Four

I turned on my small radio at around quarter to six in the evening. I had the intentions to listen to the news on top of the hour. The disc jockey belted out some zimdancehall music, one tune after another.

Suddenly there was a soft knock on the door. It was a woman's knock! I opened the door "ooh it's you Christwish! How are you?"

"I'm fine Samanyika" her mellifluous voice was well tuned. She smiled broadly towards me, "I'm so sorry for disturbing you. Well, Samaz, my gas stove isn't working properly, Shylet referred me to you."

"Okay, how much do you want to pay for the service?" I enquired jocundly.

She giggled, "any amount commensurate with the service sir." she laughed.

"Okay my dear. I'm coming to your place. Let me check for my spanner." I said. Servicing gas stoves isn't a big challenge to me.

I took my time in resorting the stove proficiently and methodically. We were seated in her tidy kitchenette. She was very smart. "I saw Tsvangison at your house." she said.

"Who is Tsvangison?" I asked her.

"Morgie!" We both bursted into a laughter. "He approached me too, but where on earth can I find such an amount of money to buy his tablet. He sleepwalked! His wife has recently packed, she couldn't resist the hunger."

"It's pathetic."

"But I think those who assaulted him during election brouhaha damaged his head."

"Ooh! That's why he bears that scar on his forehead!"

"Yes" she replied shortly. She took a moment and said, "That's why I loathe politics. Morgan was beaten nearly to death. The assailants didn't heed Morgan Tsvangirai and Robert Mugabe's peace preaching's. He was assaulted for his affiliation to the opposition party, yet a person is free to opt for his or her own political party. Violence is not the Panacea."

Suddenly I stopped screwing the stove and watched her without saying anything for a moment, then sighed, "You're right but we don't have to exonerate the opposition party. They also have some elements who perpetrate violence against the ruling party supporters. That's bad!" I barked. I also have a nephew who was heavily assaulted with planks for his affiliation to Mugabe. There is a reflect of lack of political tolerance between Zanu pf and MDC supporters. During a political brouhaha it's very deplorable that some people are displaced from their homes on the mere basis of their political opinions and affiliations in violation of the constitution which guarantees every citizen's right to assemble freely and initiate or belong to political parties of their choice. Unaware of one's rights is just as good as sleepwalking!

Suddenly her cellphone rang - and went on ringing. "Why aren't you picking your call?" Curiously I asked her.

"He is abusive and promiscuous!" The tone of her voice also told me that something somewhere was wrong, terribly wrong.

It rang inside my mind that one thing that save fake lovers from bitterness towards each other, is when they both realise how incompatible they're before plunging into marriage which others prefer to term *'jail'* nowadays. Imprisonment! I thought, finding a mutual and real life partner needs a time investment. "What happened Christwish?" I asked almost imploringly.

She looked up, her marvellous eyes shining as if she was pretty close to tears. She shook her head, came around the chair besides me and sank down into it. I had the feeling; she was trying to be brave. "I just want to relax and rest, let myself go for some time. You know what Samaz? I got the wind of his double dealings! So I'm considering terminating the relationship. I'm unlike those slumber girls who just somnolently plunge themselves into marriage. I deserve a serious God fearing and caring man" she said.

"Where did you meet this goat?"

"On Facebook."

I stared at her, but said nothing. Why using social media dating sites? I didn't ask her though. She looked bored and fed-up. Her phone started ringing again, but this time it was a private number. It went on ringing unattended. "I hadn't suspected such a scenario. Our elders said *'One thread for the needle, one love for the heart'* if he has multiple hearts then he's not the right one" I said and tried not to sound too dry and sardonic.

I couldn't help thinking that a lot of people in some relationships are busy labouring under a cloud of dissatisfaction, but still they just get into marriage unconsciously, only to wake up when mishaps exacerbates. Why people are entering into marriages with grieving hearts? Someone I couldn't remember had once said, "if not compatible, a break up before marriage hurts but heals and worth it" surely , breaking up with future *imprisonment* is painful and at that time you can feel as if an icy hand had taken hold of your heart in an inexorable cold grip, but it's worth it. You heal; henceforth look forward to a perfect suitor just as a hungry man looks forward to a good meal after gulping a glass of sherry. Literally there are suitable ones, those who possess a certain love that ooze from every open pore in their bodies unlike the *prison cell* ones. Nevertheless one has to guard against being smitten to the extent of turning on blind eyes and deaf ears to their partner's serious imperfections, behaviour wise, as the fissures jeopardises the future of the union. I've seen marriages culminating in bitter and acrimonious divorces.

Some men usually slumber by making goddesses out of women yet they're just human like us after all, mortals made of the same corruptible clay just like everybody else, contrary to all romantic idealism which has promoted the prevailing promiscuity.

There're also those of instant cohabitations as if marriages were a cerevita porridge. They date in a bus today and could cohabitate by the end of that journey. It's extremely ignominious. Waiting before taking the marriage plunge is laudable. Couples who knew each other very well at the time of marriage are at less stake than the *cerevitas*. Four days of dating are more enough for others but it culminate in disheartening consequences. Some spend huge sums of money, acquired through bank loans on weddings, but if miscalculated it can in turn ruin the institution havoc. It's better to spend not too much. A wedding isn't meant to be a show off platform. The irony of it, is that, those who date for only two weeks are the ones splashing cash and having expensive white weddings of extraordinary ways, but the couple tend to divorce too earlier. When trying to make a post-mortem through counting the days the marriage lasted ... One could count the days it survived on the fingers on one hand and actually remain with some change. It's pathetic!

I wished that day that all sleepwalkers be struck down by a bolt of God's white light, exactly the same it did to Saul of Damascus. It's high time to wake up and look all our demons straight in the eye.
I look forward to a blessed Sunday though.

THE END

www.ingramcontent.com/pod-product-compliance
Lightning Source LLC
Chambersburg PA
CBHW031322060726
47590CB00003B/1310